THE
MARS GIRL

JOE HALDEMAN

an imprint of

ARC
MANOR

Rockville, Maryland

Tarikian, TARK Classic Fiction, Arc Manor, Arc Manor Classic Reprints, Phoenix Pick, Phoenix Science Fiction Classics, Phoenix Rider, The Stellar Guild Series, Manor Thrift and logos associated with those imprints are trademarks or registered trademarks of Arc Manor, LLC, Rockville, Maryland. All other trademarks and trademarked names are properties of their respective owners.

Book design concept by Lezli Robyn

ISBN: 978-1-61242-316-6

www.PhoenixPick.com
Great Science Fiction & Fantasy
Free Ebook Every Month

Published by Phoenix Pick
an imprint of Arc Manor
P. O. Box 10339
Rockville, MD 20849-0339
www.ArcManor.com

1. GOODBYE, COOL WORLD

The space elevator is the only elevator in the world with barf bags. My brother Card pointed that out. He notices things like that; I noticed the bathroom. One bathroom, for forty-some people. Locked in an elevator for two weeks. It's not as big as it looks in the advertisements.

It wasn't too bad, actually, once we started going up. Nothing like the old-fashioned way of getting into orbit, strapped to a million pounds of high explosive. We lost weight slowly during the week it took us to get to the Orbit Hilton, where we were weightless. We dropped off a dozen or so rich tourists there (and spent a couple of hours and no money, looking around) and then continued crawling up the Elevator for another week, to where our Mars ship the *John Carter* was parked, waiting.

The newsies called it "Kids in Space," hand me a barf bag. The Mars colony had like seventy-five people, aged from the early thirties to the late sixties, and they wanted to add some young people. They set up a lottery among scientists and engineers with children age nine and older, and my parents were among the nine couples chosen, so they dragged me (Carmen Dula) and Card along.

Card thought it was wonderful, and I'll admit I thought it was spec, too, at the time. So Card and I got to spend a year of Saturday mornings training to take the test—just us; there was no test for parents. Adults make it or they don't, depending on things like education. Our parents have enough education for any dozen normal people.

These tests were basically to make *us* seem normal, or at least normal enough not to go detroit locked up in a sardine can with twenty-nine other people for six months.

So here's the billion-dollar question: Did any of the kids aboard pass the tests just because they actually were normal? Or did all of them also give up a year of Saturdays so they could learn how to hide their homicidal tendencies from the testers?

And the trillion-dollar question is "What was I *thinking?*" We had to stay on Mars a minimum of five years. I would be twenty-one, having pissed away my precious teenage years on a rusty airless rock.

So anyhow. Going aboard the good ship *John Carter* were seven boys and seven girls, along with their eighteen parents and one sort of attractive pilot, Paul Santos, not quite twice my age.

I just turned sixteen but am starting college. Which I'll attend by virtual reality and email. No wicked fraternity parties, no experimenting with drugs and sex and finding out how much beer you can hold before overflowing. Maybe this whole Mars thing was a ruse my parents made up to keep me off campus. My education was going to be so incomplete!

The living area of the *John Carter* was huge, compared to the Elevator. We had separate areas for study and exercise and meals, and a sleeping floor away from the parents, as long as we behaved. I roomed with my best friends aboard, Elspeth and Kaimei, from Israel and California.

We spent the first couple of hours strapped in, up in the lander on top of the ship. Most of the speed we needed for getting to Mars was "free"—when we left the high orbit at the end of the Space Elevator, we were like a stone thrown from an old-fashioned sling, or a bit of mud flung from a bicycle tire. Two weeks of relatively slow crawling built up into one big boost, from the orbit of Earth to the orbit of Mars.

We started out strapped in because there were course corrections, all automatic. The ship studied our progress and then pointed in different directions and made small bursts of thrust, which Paul studied but didn't correct. Then we unstrapped and floated back to the artificial gravity of the rotating living area.

It would take six months to get to Mars, most of it schoolwork and exercising. I started class at the University of Maryland in the second week.

I was not the most popular girl in my classes—I wasn't *in* class at all, of course, except as a face in a cube. As we moved away from Earth and the time delay grew longer, it became impossible for me to respond in real time to what was going on. So if I had questions to ask, I had to time it so I was asking them at the beginning of class the next day.

That's a prescription for making yourself a tiresome know-it-all bitch. I had all day to think about the questions and look stuff up. So I was always thoughtful and relevant and a tiresome know-it-all bitch. Of course it didn't help at all that I was younger than everybody else and a brave pioneer headed for another planet. The novelty of that wore off real fast.

Card wasn't having any such problems. But he already knew most of his classmates, some of them since grade school, and was more social anyhow. I've always been the youngest in my class, and the brain.

It's not as if anybody had forced me into the situation. I was bored as hell in grade school and middle school, and when I was given the option of testing out of a grade and skipping ahead, I did it, three times. Not a big problem when you're eight and ten and twelve. It *is* a problem when you're barely sixteen and everybody else is "college age," at least by the calendar.

I'm also a little behind them socially, or a lot behind. I had male friends but didn't date much. Still a virgin, technically, and when I'm around older kids feel like I'm wearing a sign proclaiming that fact.

That raised an interesting possibility. I never could see myself still a virgin at twenty-one. I might wind up being the first girl to lose it on Mars—or on any other planet at all. Maybe some day they'd put up a plaque: "In this storage room on such-and-such a date…"

About a month out, we developed a little problem, that we hoped wouldn't kill everybody more or less slowly. The ship started losing air, slowly but surely. We found out it was leaking out of the lander, but couldn't find the leak. So we just closed the airlock between the lander and the living quarters.

Paul was not happy about that, having to run things away from his pilot's console, using a laptop. But it wasn't like he had to steer around asteroids or anything.

The six months actually went by pretty fast. You might think that being locked up in a space ship would drive people crazy, but in fact it seemed to drive them sane, even the youngest. The idea of "Spaceship Earth" is such an old cliché that Granddad makes a face at it. But being constantly aware that we were isolated, surrounded by space, did seem to make us more considerate of one another. So if Earth is just a bigger ship, why couldn't they learn to be as virtuous as we are? Maybe they don't choose their crew carefully enough.

Anyhow, Mars became the brightest star, and then a little circle, and then a planet. We pumped air back into the lander and left our home there in orbit. Some people took pills as they strapped in. I wasn't that smart.

2. DOWN TO MARS

Someday, maybe before I'm dead, Mars will have its own Space Elevator, but until then people have to get down there the old-fashioned way, in space-shuttle mode. It's like the difference between taking an elevator from the top floor of a building, or jumping off with an umbrella and a prayer. Fast and terrifying.

We'd lived with the lander as part of our home for weeks, and then as a mysterious kind of threatening presence, airless and waiting. Most of us weren't eager to go into it.

Before we'd made our second orbit of Mars, Paul opened the inner door, prepared to crack the airlock, and said, "Let's go."

We'd been warned, so we were bundled up against the sudden temperature drop when the airlock opened, and were not surprised that our ears popped painfully. But then we had to take our little metal suitcases and float through the airlock to go strap into our assigned seats, and try not to shit while we dropped like a rock to our doom.

From my studies I knew that the lander loses velocity by essentially trading speed for heat—hitting the thin Martian atmosphere at a drastic angle so the ship heats up to cherry red. What the diagrams in the physical science book don't show is the tooth-rattling vibration, the bucking and gut-wrenching wobble. If I'm never that scared again in my life I'll be really happy.

All of the violence stopped abruptly when the lander decided to become a glider, I guess a few hundred miles from the landing strip. I wished we had windows like a regular airplane, but then realized that might be asking for a heart attack. It was scary enough just to squint at Paul's two-foot-wide screen as the ground rose up to meet us, too steep and fast to believe.

We landed on skis, grating and rumbling along the rocky ground. They'd moved all the big rocks out of our way, but we felt every one of the small ones. Paul had warned us to keep our tongues away from our teeth, which was a good thing. It could be awkward, starting out life on a new planet unable to speak because you've bitten off your tongue.

We hadn't put on the Mars suits for the flight down; they were too bulky to fit in the close-ranked seats—and I guess there wasn't any disaster scenario where we would still be alive and need them. So the first order of the day was to get dressed for our new planet.

We'd tested them several times, but Paul wanted to be super-cautious the first time they were actually exposed to the Martian near-vacuum. The airlock would only hold two people at once, so we went out one at a time, with Paul observing us, ready to toss us back inside if trouble developed.

We unpacked the suits from storage under the deck and sorted them out. One for each person and two blobby general-purpose ones.

We were to leave in reverse alphabetical order, which was no fun, since it made our family dead last. The lander had never felt particularly claustrophobic before, but now it was like a tiny tin can, the sardines slowly exiting one by one.

At least we could see out, via the pilot's screen. He'd set the camera on the base, where all seventy-five people had gathered to watch us land, or crash. That led to some morbid speculation on Card's part. What if we'd crash-landed *into* them? I guess we'd be just as likely to crash into the base behind them. I'd rather be standing outside with a space suit on, too.

We'd seen pictures of the base a million times, not to mention endless diagrams and descriptions of how everything worked, but it was kind of exciting to see it in real time, to actually be here. The farm part looked bigger than I'd pictured it, I guess because the people standing around gave it scale. Of course the people lived underneath, staying out of the radiation.

It was interesting to have actual gravity. I said it felt different and Mom agreed, with a scientific explanation. Residual centripetal blah blah blah. I'll just call it real gravity, as opposed to the manufactured kind. Organic gravity.

A lot of people undressed on the spot and got into their Mars suits. I didn't see any point in standing around for an hour in the thing. I'm also a little shy, in a selective way. I waited until Paul was on the other side of the airlock before I revealed my un-voluptuous figure and barely necessary bra. Which I'd have to take off anyhow, for the skinsuit part of the Mars suit.

That part was like a lightweight body stocking. It fastened up the front with a gecko strip and then you pushed a button on your wrist and something electrical happened and it clasped your body like a big rubber glove. It could be sexy-looking if your body was. Most people looked like big gray cartoons, the men with a little more detail than I wanted to see.

The outer part of the Mars suit was more like lightweight armor, kind of loose and clanky when you put it on, but it also did an electrical thing when you zipped up, and fit more closely. Then clumsy boots and gloves and a helmet, all airtight. The joints would sigh when you moved your arms or legs or bent at the waist.

Card's suit had a place for an extension at the waist, since he could grow as much as a foot taller while we were here. Mine didn't have any such refinement, though the chest part was optimistically roomy.

Since we did follow strict anti-alphabetical order, Card got the distinction of being the last one out, and I was next to last. I got in the airlock with Paul, and he checked my oxygen tanks and the seals on my helmet, gloves, and boots. Then he pumped most of the air out, watching the clock, and asked me to count even numbers backward from thirty. (I asked him whether he had an obsession with backward lists.) He smiled at me through the helmet and kept his hand on my shoulder as the rest of the air pumped out and the door silently swung open.

The sky was brighter than I'd expected, and the ground darker. "Welcome to Mars," Paul said on the suit radio, sounding really far away.

We walked down a metal ramp to the sandy rock-strewn ground. I stepped onto another planet.

How many people had ever done that?

Everything was suddenly different. This was the most real thing I'd ever done.

They could talk until they were blue in the face about how special this was, brave new frontier, leaving the cradle of Earth, whatever, and it's finally just words. When I felt the crunch of Martian soil under my boot it was suddenly all very plain and wonderful. I remembered an old cube—a movie—of one of the first guys on the Moon, jumping around like a little kid, and I jumped myself, and again, way high.

"Careful!" came Paul's voice over the radio. "Get used to it first."

"Okay, okay." While I walked, feather light, toward the other airlock, I tried to figure out how many people had actually done it, set foot on another world. A little more than a hundred, in all of history. And me one of them, now.

There were four people waiting at the airlock door; everyone else had gone inside. I looked around at the rusty desert and stifled the urge to run off and explore—I mean, for more than three months we hadn't been able to go more than a few dozen feet in any direction, and here was a whole new world. But there would be time. Soon!

Mother was blinking away tears, unable to touch her face behind the helmet, crying with happiness. The dream of her lifetime. I hugged her, which felt strange, both of us swaddled in insulation. Our helmets clicked together and for a moment I heard her laugh.

While Paul went back to get Card, I just looked around. I'd spent hours there in virtual, of course, but that was fake. This was hard-edged and strange, even fearsome in a way. A desert with rocks. Yellow sky of air so thin it would kill you in a breath.

When Card got to the ground, he jumped higher than I had. Paul grabbed him by the arm and walked him over.

The airlock held four people. Paul and the two strangers gestured for us to go in when the door opened. It closed automatically behind us and a red light throbbed for about a minute. I could hear the muffled clicking of a pump. Then a green light and the inside door sighed open.

We stepped into the greenhouse, a dense couple of acres of grain and vegetables and dwarf fruit trees. A woman in shorts and a T-shirt motioned for us to take off our helmets.

She introduced herself as Emily. "I keep track of the airlock and suits," she said. "Follow me and we'll get you square."

Feeling overdressed, we clanked down a metal spiral stair to a room full of shelves and boxes, the walls unpainted rock. One block of metal shelves was obviously for our crew, names written on bright new tape under shelves that held folded Mars suits and the titanium suitcases.

"Just come on through to the mess hall after you're dressed," she said. "Place isn't big enough to get lost. Not yet." They planned to more than double the underground living area while we were here.

I helped Mother out of her suit and she helped me. I needed a shower and some clean clothes. My jumpsuit was wrinkled and damp with old sweat, fear sweat from the landing. I didn't smell like a petunia myself. But we were all in the same boat.

Paul and the two other men in Mars suits were rattling down the stairs as we headed for the mess hall. The top half of the corridor was smooth plastic that radiated uniform dim light, like the tubes that had linked the Space Elevator to the Hilton and the *John Carter*. The bottom half was numbered storage drawers.

I knew what to expect of the mess hall and the other rooms; the colony was a series of inflated half-cylinders inside a large irregular tunnel, a natural pipe through an ancient lava flow. Someday the whole thing would be closed off and filled with air like the part we'd just left, but for the time being everyone lived and worked in the reinforced balloons.

It all seemed pretty huge after living in a space ship. I don't suppose it would be that imposing if you went there directly from a town or a city on Earth.

The mess hall wasn't designed for everyone to crowd in there at once. Most of the colonists were standing around at the far end. There were two dining tables with plenty of empty chairs for us new people. We sat down, I guess all of us feeling a little awkward. Everybody sort of staring and nodding. We hadn't seen a stranger since the Hilton—but then none of these Martians had seen a new person since the last ship, fifteen months before.

I looked through the crowd and immediately picked out Oz. He gave me a little wave and I returned it.

The room had two large false windows, like the ones on the ship, looking out onto the desert. I assumed they were real-time. Nothing was moving, but then all the life on the planet was presumably right here.

You could see our lander sitting at the end of a mile-long plowed groove. I wondered whether Paul had cut it too close, stopping a couple of hundred feet away. He'd said the landing was mostly automatic, but I didn't see him let go of the joystick.

There was a carafe of water on the table, and some glasses. I poured half a glass, careful not to spill any, feeling everybody's eyes on me. Water was precious here, at least for the time being.

When Paul and the other two came into the room, an older woman stepped forward. Like many of them, men and women, she was wearing a belted robe made of some filmy material. She was pale and bony.

"Welcome to Mars. Of course I've spoken with most of you. I'm Dargo Solingen, current general administrator.

"The first couple of ares"—Martian days—"you are here, just settle in and get used to your new home. Explore and ask questions. We've assigned temporary living and working spaces to everyone, a compromise between the wish list you sent a couple of weeks ago and...reality." She shrugged. "It will be a little tight until the new module is in place. We will start on that as soon as the ship is unloaded."

She almost smiled, though it looked like she didn't have much practice with it. "It is strange to see children. It will be an interesting social experiment."

"One you don't quite approve of?" Dr. Jefferson said.

"You may as well know that I don't. But I was not consulted."

"Dr. Solingen," a woman behind her said in a tone of warning.

"I guess none of you were," he said. "It was an Earth decision."

Oz stepped forward. "We were polled. Most of us were very much in favor."

The woman who had cautioned Solingen joined him. "A hundred percent of the permanent party. Those of us who are not returning to Earth." She was either pregnant or the only fat person in the room. Looking more carefully, I saw one other woman who appeared to be pregnant.

You'd think that would have been on the news. Maybe it was and I missed it, not likely. Mother and I exchanged significant glances. Something was going on.

3. MOVING IN

It turned out to be nothing more mysterious than a desire for privacy on the women's part, and everybody's desire to keep Earth out of their hair. When the first child was born, the Earth press would be all over them. Until then, there was no need for anyone to know the blessed event was nigh. So they asked that we not mention the pregnancies when writing or talking to home.

I shared a small room with Elspeth and Kaimei—an air mattress on the floor and a bunk bed. We agreed to rotate, so everyone would have an actual bed two-thirds of the time.

There was only one desk, with a small screen and a clunky keyboard and an old VR helmet with a big dent on the side. The timing for that worked out okay, since Elspeth had classes seven hours before Eastern time, and Kaimei three hours later. We drew up a chart and taped it to the wall. The only conflict was my physical science class versus Kaimei's History of Tao and Buddhism. Mine was mostly equations on the board, so I used the screen and let her have the helmet.

Our lives were pretty regimented the first couple of weeks, because we had to coordinate classes with the work roster here, and leave a little time for eating and sleeping.

Everybody was impatient to get the new module set up, but it wasn't just a matter of unloading and inflating it. First there was a light exoskeleton of spindly metal rods that became rigid when they were all pulled together. Then floorboards to bear the weight of the things and people inside. Then the connection to the existing base, through an improvised airlock until they were sure the module wouldn't leak.

I enjoyed working on that, at first outdoors, unloading the ship and sorting and pre-assembling some parts; then later, down in the lava cave, attaching the new to the old. I got used to working in the Mars suit and using the "dog," a wheeled machine about the size of a large dog. It carried backup oxygen and power.

About half the time, though, my work roster put me inside, helping the younger ones do their lessons and avoid boredom. "Mentoring," they called it, to make it sound more important than babysitting.

One day, though, while I was just getting off work detail, Paul came up and asked whether I'd like to go exploring with him. What, skip math? I got fresh oxygen and helped him check out one of the dogs and we went for a walk.

The surface of Mars might look pretty boring to an outsider, but it's not at all. It must be the same if you live in a desert on Earth: you pretty much have the space around your home memorized, every little mound and rock—and when you venture out it's "Wow! A different rock!"

He took me off to the left of Telegraph Hill, walking at a pretty good pace. The base was below the horizon in less than ten minutes. We were still in radio contact as long as we could see the antenna on top of the hill, and if we wanted to go farther, the dog had a collapsible booster antenna that went up ten meters, which we could leave behind as a relay.

We didn't need it for that, but Paul clicked it up into place when we came to the edge of a somewhat deep crater he wanted to climb into.

"Be really careful," he said. "We have to leave the dog behind. If we both were to fall and be injured, we'd be in deep shit."

I followed him, watching carefully as we picked our way to the top. Once there, he turned around and pointed.

It's hard to really say how strange the sight was. We weren't that high up, but you could see the curvature of the horizon. To the right of Telegraph Hill, the gleam of the greenhouse roof. The dog behind us looked tiny but unnaturally clear, in the near vacuum.

Paul was carrying a white bag, now a little rust-streaked from the dust. He pulled out a photo-map of the crater, unfolded it, and showed it to me. There were about twenty X's, starting on the top of the crater rim, where we must have been standing, then down the incline, and across the crater floor to its central peak.

"Dust collecting," he said. "How's your oxygen?"

I chinned the readout button. "Three hours forty minutes."

"That should be plenty. Now you don't have to go down if you—"

"I do! Let's go!"

"Okay. Follow me." I didn't tell him that my impatience wasn't all excitement, but partly anxiety at having to talk and pee at the same time. Peeing standing up, into a diaper, trying desperately not to fart. "Funny as a fart in a space suit" probably goes back to the beginning of space flight, but there's nothing real funny about it in reality. I'd taken two anti-gas tablets before I came out, and they seemed to still be working.

Keeping your footing was a little harder, going downhill. Paul had the map folded over so it only showed the path down the crater wall; every thirty or forty steps he would fish through the bag and take out a pre-labeled plastic vial, and scrape a sample of dirt into it.

On the floor of the crater I felt a little shiver of fear at our isolation. Looking back the way we'd come, though, I could see the tip of the dog's antenna.

The dust was deeper than I'd seen anyplace else, I guess because the crater walls kept out the wind. Paul took two samples as we walked toward the central peak.

"You better stay down here, Carmen. I won't be long." The peak was steep, and he scrambled up it like a monkey. I wanted to yell "Be careful," but kept my mouth shut.

Looking up at him, the sun behind me, I could see Earth gleaming blue in the ochre sky. How long had it been since I thought of Earth, other than "the place where school is"? I guess I hadn't been here long enough to feel homesickness. Nostalgia for Earth—crowded place with lots of gravity and heat.

It might be the first time I seriously thought about staying. In five years I'd be twenty-one and Paul would still be under forty. I didn't feel romantic about him, but I liked him and he was funny. That would put us way ahead of a lot of marriages I'd observed.

Romance was for movies and books, anyhow. When actual people you know started acting that way, they were so ridiculous.

But then how did I really feel about Paul? Up there being heroic and competent and, admit it, sexy.

Turn down the heat, girl. He's only twelve years younger than your father, Probably sterile from radiation, too. I didn't think I wanted children, but it would be nice to have the option.

He collected his samples and tossed the bag down. It drifted slowly, rotating, and landed about ten feet away. I was enough of a Martian to be surprised to hear a click when it landed, the soles of my boots picking the noise up, conducted through the rock of the crater floor.

He worked his way down slowly, which was a relief. I was holding the sample bag; he took it and I followed him back the way we had come.

At the top of the crater wall, he stopped and looked back. "Can't see it from here," he said. "I'll show you."

"What?"

"My greatest triumph," he said, and started down. "You'll be impressed."

He didn't offer any further explanation on the ground. He picked up the dog's handle and proceeded to walk around to the other side of the crater.

It was a dumbo, an unpiloted supply vehicle. Its rear end was tilted up, the nose down in a small crater.

"I brought her in lik.e that. I was not the most popular man on Mars." As we approached it, I could see the ragged hole someone had cut in the side with a torch or a laser. "Landed it right on the bay door, too."

"Wow. I'm glad you weren't hurt."

He laughed. "It was remote control; I landed it from a console inside the base. Harder than being aboard, actually." We turned around and headed back to the base.

"It was a judgment call. There was a lot of variable wind, and it was yawing back and forth." He made a hand motion like a fish swimming. "I was sort of trying not to hit the base or Telegraph Hill. But I overdid it."

"People could understand that."

"Understanding isn't forgiving. Everybody had to stop their science and become pack animals." I could see the expression on Solingen's face, having to do labor, and smiled.

She really had something against me. I had to do twice as much babysitting as Elspeth or Kaimei—and when I suggested that the boys ought to do it, too, she said that "personnel allocation" was *her* job, thank you. And when my person got allocated to an outside job, it would be something boring and repetitive, like taking inventory of supplies. (That was especially useful, in case there were Martians sneaking in at night to steal nuts and bolts.)

When we got back, I went straight to the console and found a blinking note from the Dragon herself, noting that I had missed math class, saying she wanted a copy of my homework. Did she monitor anybody else's VR attendance?

I'd had the class recorded, of course, the super-exciting chain rule for differentiation. I fell asleep twice, hard to do in

VR, and had to start over. Then I had a problem set with fifty chains to differentiate. Wrap me in chains and throw me in the differential dungeon, but I had to sleep. I got the air mattress partly inflated and flopped onto it without undressing.

Not delivering my homework like a good little girl got me into a special corner of Dargo Hell. I had to turn over my notes and homework in maths every day to Ana Sitral, who obviously didn't have time for checking it. She must have done something to piss off the Dragon herself.

Then I had to take on over half of the mentoring hours that Kaimei and Elspeth had been covering, and was not allowed any outside time. I had been selfish, Dargo said, tiring myself out on a silly lark, using up resources that might be needed for real work. So I had the temerity to suggest that part of my real work was getting to know Mars, and she really blew up about that. It was not up to me to make up my own training schedule.

Okay, part of it was that she didn't like kids. But part was also that she didn't like *me*, and wouldn't if I was a hundred years old. She didn't bother to hide that from anybody. I complained to Mother and she didn't disagree, but said I had to learn to work with people like that. Especially here, where there wasn't much choice.

I didn't bother complaining to Dad. He would make a Growth Experience out of it. I should try to see the world her way. Sorry, Dad. If I saw the world her way and thought about Carmen Dula, wouldn't that be self-loathing? That would not be a positive growth experience.

4. FISH OUT OF WATER

After a month, I was able to put a Mars suit on again, but I didn't go up to the surface. There was plenty of work down below, inside the lava tube that protected the base from cosmic and solar radiation.

There's plenty of water on Mars, but most of it is in the wrong place. If it was on or near the surface, it had to be at the north or south pole. We couldn't put bases there, because they were in total darkness a lot of the time, and we needed solar power.

But there was a huge lake hidden more than a kilometer below the base. It was the easiest one to get to on all of Mars, we learned from some kind of satellite radar, which was why the base was put here. One of the things we'd brought on the *John Carter* was a drilling system designed to tap it. (The drills that came with the first ship and the third broke, though, the famous Mars Luck.)

I worked with the team that set the drill up, nothing more challenging than fetch-and-carry, but a lot better than trying to mentor kids when you wanted to slap them instead.

*F*or a while we could hear the drill, a faint sandpapery sound that was conducted through the rock. Then it was quiet, and most of us forgot about it. A few weeks later, though, it was Sagan 12th, which from then on would be Water Day.

We put on Mars suits and then walked down between the wall of the lava tube and the base's exterior wall. It was kind of creepy, just suit lights, less than a meter between the cold rock and the inflated plastic you weren't supposed to touch.

Then there was light ahead, and we came out into swirling madness—it was a blizzard! The drill had struck water and sent it up under pressure, several liters a minute. When it hit the cold vacuum it exploded into snow.

It was ankle-deep in places, but of course it wouldn't last; the vacuum would evaporate it eventually. But people were already working with lengths of pipe, getting ready to fill the waiting tanks up in the hydroponics farm. One of them had already been dubbed the swimming pool. And that's how the trouble started.

I got on the work detail that hooked the water supply up to the new pump. That was to go in two stages: emergency and "maintenance."

The emergency stage worked on the reasonable assumption that the pump wasn't going to last very long. So we wanted to save every drop of water we could, while it still did work.

This was the "water boy" stage. We had collapsible insulated water containers that held fifty liters each. That's 110 pounds on Earth, about my own weight, awkward but not too heavy to handle on Mars.

All ten of the older kids spent a couple of hours on duty, a couple off, doing water boy. We had wheelbarrows, three of them, so it wasn't too tiring. You fill the thing with water, which takes eight minutes, then turn off the valve and get away fast, so not too much pressure builds up before the next person takes over. Then trundle the wheelbarrow around to the airlock, leave it there, and carry or drag the water bag across the farm to the storage tanks. Dump in the water—a slurry of ice by then—and go back to the pump with your wheelbarrow.

The work was boring as dust, and would drive you insane if you didn't have music. I started out being virtuous, listening to classical pieces that went along with a book on the history of music. But as the days droned by, I listened to more and more city and even sag.

You didn't have to be a math whiz to see that it was going to take three weeks at this rate to fill the first tank, which was two meters tall and eight meters wide, bigger than some backyard pools in Florida.

The water didn't stay icy; they warmed it up to above room temperature. We all must have fantasized about diving in there and paddling around. Elspeth and Kaimei and I even planned for it.

There was no sense in asking permission from the Dragon. What we were going to do was coordinate our showers so we'd all be squeaky clean—so nobody could say we were contaminating the water supply—and come in the same time, off shift, and see whether we could get away with a little skinny-dip. Or see how long we could do it before somebody stopped us.

At two weeks, the engineers sort of forced our hand. They'd been working on a direct link from the pump to this tank and the other two.

Jordan Westling, Barry's inventor dad, seemed to be in charge of that team. We always got along pretty well. He was old but always had a twinkle in his eye.

He and I were alone by the tank while he fiddled with some tubing and gauges. I lifted the water bag with a groan and poured it in.

"This ought to be the last day you have to do that," he said. "We should be on line in a few hours."

"Wow." I stepped up on a box and looked at the water level. It was more than half full, with a little layer of red sediment at the bottom. "Dr. Westling...what would happen if somebody went swimming in this?"

He didn't look up from the gauge. "I suppose if somebody washed up first and didn't pee in the pool, nobody would have to know. It's not exactly distilled water. Not that I would endorse such an activity."

When I went back to the water point I touched helmets with Kaimei—that way you can talk without using the suit radio, which is probably monitored—and we agreed we'd do it at 02:15, just after the end of the next shift. She'd pass the word on to Elspeth, who came on at midnight. That would give her time to have a quick shower and smuggle a towel up to the tank.

I got off at 10 and VR'ed a class on Spinoza, better than any sleeping pill. I barely stayed awake long enough to set the alarm for 1:30.

Two and a half hours' sleep was plenty. I awoke with eager anticipation and, alone in the room, put on a robe and slippers and quietly made my way to the shower.

Kaimei had already bathed, and was sitting outside the shower with a reader. I took my two-liter shower and, while I was drying, Elspeth came in from work, wearing skinsuit and socks.

After she showered, the three of us tiptoed past the work/study area—a couple of people were working there, but a hanging partition kept them from being distracted by passersby.

The mess hall was deserted. We went up through the changing room and the airlock foyer and slipped into the farm.

There were only dim maintenance lights at this hour. We padded our way to the swimming pool tank—and heard whispered voices!

Oscar Jefferson, Barry Westling, and my idiot brother had beat us to it!

"Hey girls," Oscar said. "Look—we're out of a job." A faucet in the side was gurgling out a narrow stream.

"My father said we could quit," Barry said, "so we thought we'd take a swim to celebrate."

"You didn't tell him," I said."

"Do we look like idiots?" No, they looked like naked boys. "Come on in. The water's not too cold."

I looked at the other two girls and they shrugged okay. Space ships and Mars bases don't give you a lot of room for modesty.

I sort of liked the way Barry looked at me anyhow, when I stepped out of my robe and slippers. When Kaimei undressed, his look might have been a little more intense.

I stepped up on the box and had one leg over the edge of the tank when the lights snapped on full.

"Caught you!" Dargo Solingen marched down the aisle between the tomatoes and the squash. "I *knew* you'd do this." She looked at me, one foot on the box and the other dangling in space. "And I know exactly who the ringleader is."

She stood with her hands on her hips, studying. Elspeth was only half undressed, but the rest of us were obviously ready for some teenaged sex orgy. "Get out, now. Get dressed and come to my office at 0800. We will have a disciplinary hearing." She stomped back to the door and snapped off the bright lights on her way out.

"I'll tell her it wasn't you," Card said. "We just kind of all decided when Barry's dad said the thing was working."

"She won't believe you," I said, stepping down. "She's been after my ass all along."

"Who wouldn't be?" Barry said, studying the subject. He was such a born romantic.

All of our parents were crowded into the Dragon's office at 0800. That was not good. My parents both were working the shift from 2100 to 0400, and needed their sleep. The parents were on one side of the room, and we were on the other, separated by a large video screen.

Without any preamble, Dargo Solingin made the charge: "Last night your children went for a swim in the new Water Tank One. Tests on the water reveal traces of coliform bacteria, so it cannot be used for human consumption without boiling or some other form of sterilization."

"It was only going to be used for hydroponics," Dr. Westling said.

"You can't say that for certain. At any rate, it was an act of extreme irresponsibility, and one that you encouraged." She pointed a hand control at the video screen and clicked. I saw myself talking to him.

"What would happen if somebody went swimming in this?" He answered that nobody would have to know—not that he would endorse such a thing. He was restraining a smile.

"You're secretly recording me?" he said incredulously.

"Not you. Her."

"She didn't do it!" Card blurted out. "It was my idea."

"You will speak when spoken to," she said coldly. "Your loyalty to your sister is touching, but misplaced." She clicked again, and there was a picture of me and Kaimei at the water point, touching helmets.

"Tonight has to be skinny-dipping night. Dr. Westling says they'll be on line in a few hours. Let's make it 0215, right after Elspeth gets off." You could hear Kaimei's faint agreement.

"You had my daughter's suit bugged?" my father said.

"Not really. I just disabled the OFF switch on her suit communicator."

"That is so…so illegal. On Earth they'd throw you out of court and then—"

"This isn't Earth. And on Mars, there is nothing more important than water. As you would appreciate if you had lived here as long as I have." Oh, sure. I think you could live longer without water than without air.

"Besides, it was improper for the boys and girls to be together naked. Even if they hadn't planned any sexual misbehavior—"

"Oh, please," I said. "Excuse me for speaking out of turn, Dr. Solingen, but there was nothing like that. We didn't even know the boys would be there."

"Really. The timing was remarkable, then. And you weren't acting surprised about them when I turned on the lights. Nor modest." Card was squirming, and put up his hand, but the Dragon ignored it. She turned to the parents. "I want to discuss with you what punishment might be appropriate."

"Twenty laps a day in the pool," Dr. Westling said, almost snarling. He didn't like her anyhow, I'd noticed, and spying on him apparently had been the straw that broke the camel's back. "They're just kids, for Chris'sake."

"You're going to say they didn't mean any harm. They have to learn that Mars doesn't recognize that as an excuse.

"An appropriate punishment, I think, would start with not allowing them to bathe for a month. I would also reduce the amount of water they be allowed to drink, but that is difficult to control. And I wouldn't want to endanger their health." God, she is so All Heart.

"For that month, I would also deny them recreational use of the cube and VR, and no exploring on the surface. Double that for the instigator, Ms. Dula"—and she turned back to face us—"and her brother as well, if he insists on sharing the responsibility."

"I *do*," he snapped.

"Very well. Two months for both of you."

"It seems harsh," Kaimei's father said. "Kaimei told me that the girls did take the precaution of showering before entering the water."

"Intent means nothing. The bacteria are there."

"Harmless to plants," Dr. Westling repeated.

She looked at him for a long second. "Your dissent is noted. Are there any other objections to this punishment?"

"Not the punishment," my mother said, "but Dr. Dula and I both object to the means of acquiring evidence."

"I am perfectly willing to stand on review for that." The old-timers would probably go along with her. The new ones might still be infected by the Bill of Rights, or the laws of Russia and France and Israel.

There were no other objections, so she reminded the parents that they would be responsible for monitoring our VR and cube use, but even more, she would rely on our sense of honor.

What were we supposed to be "honoring," though? The now old-fashioned sanctity of water? Her right to spy on us? In fact, her unlimited authority?

I would find a way to get back at her.

5. NIGHT WALK

After one day of steaming over it, I'd had enough. I don't know when I made the decision, or whether it even *was* a decision, rather than a kind of sleepwalking. It was sometime before three in the morning. I was still feeling so angry and embarrassed I couldn't get to sleep.

So I got up and started down the corridor to the mess hall, nibble on something. But I walked on past.

It looked like no one else was up. Just dim safety lights. I wound up in the dressing room and realized what I was doing.

Paul had shown me how to prop a pencil in the inner door so that the airlock chime wouldn't go off. With that disabled, a person could actually go outside alone, undetected. I could just be by myself for an hour or two, then sneak back in.

And did I ever want to be by myself.

I went through the dress-up procedure as quietly as possible. Then before I took a step toward the airlock, I visualized myself doing a safety check on another person and did it methodically on myself. It would be so pathetic to die out there, breaking the rules.

I went up the stairs silently as a thief. Well, I *was* a thief. What could they do, deport me?

For safety's sake, I decided to take a dog, even though it would slow me down a bit. I actually hesitated, and tested carrying two extra oxygen bottles by themselves, but that was awkward. *Better safe than sorry,* I said to myself in Mother's voice, and ground my teeth while saying it. But going out without a dog and dying would be pathetic. Arch-criminals are evil, not pathetic.

The evacuating pump sounded loud, though I knew you could hardly hear it in the changing room. It rattled off into silence, then the red light glowed green and the door swung open into darkness.

I stepped out, pulling the dog, and the door slid shut behind it.

I decided not to turn on the suit light, and stood there for several minutes while my eyes adjusted. Walking at night just by starlight—you couldn't do that any other place I've lived. It wouldn't be dangerous if I was careful. Besides, if I turned on a light, someone could see me from the mess hall window.

The nearby rocks gave me my bearings, and I started out toward Telegraph Hill. On the other side I'd be invisible from the base, and vice versa—alone for the first time in almost a year. Earth year.

Seeing the familiar rock field in this ghostly half-light brought back some of the mystery and excitement of the first couple of days. The landing and my first excursion with Paul.

If he knew I was doing this—well, he might approve, secretly. He wasn't much of a rule guy, except for safety.

Thinking that, my foot turned on a small rock and I staggered, getting my balance back. Keep your eyes on the ground while you're walking. It would be, what is the word I'm looking for, *pathetic* to trip and break your helmet out here.

It took me less than a half hour to get to the base of Telegraph Hill. It wasn't all that steep, but the dog's traction wasn't really up to it. A truly adventurous person would leave the dog behind and climb to the top with her suit air alone, and although I do like adventure, I'm also afflicted with pa-thetico-phobia. The dog and I could go around the mountain rather than over it. I decided to walk in a straight line for one hour, see how far I could get, and walk back.

That was my big mistake. One of them, anyhow. If I'd just gone to the top, taken a picture, and headed straight back, I might have gotten away with it.

I wasn't totally stupid. I didn't go into the hill's "radio shadow," and I cranked the dog's radio antenna up all the way, since I was headed for the horizon, and knew that any small depression in the ground could hide me from the colony's radio transceiver.

The wind picked up a little. I couldn't feel or hear it, of course, but the sky showed it. Jupiter was just rising, and its bright pale yellow light had a halo, and was slightly dimmed, by the dust in the air. I remembered Dad pointing out Jupiter, and then Mars, the morning we left Florida, and had a deli-cious shiver at the thought that I was standing on that little point of light now.

The area immediately around the colony was as well ex-plored as any place on Mars, but I knew from rock-hounding with Paul that you could find new stuff just a couple hundred meters from the airlock door. I went four or five kilometers, and found something really new.

I had been going for 57 minutes, about to turn back, and was looking for a soft rock that I could mark with an X or something—maybe scratch SURRENDER, PUNY EARTHLINGS on it, though I suspected people would figure out who had done it.

There was no noise. Just a suddenly weightless feeling, and I was falling through a hole in the ground—I'd broken through something like a thin sheet of ice. But there was nothing underneath it!

I was able to turn on the suit light as I tumbled down, but all I saw was a glimpse of the dog spinning around beside and then above me.

It seemed like a long time, but I guess I didn't fall for more than a few seconds. I hit hard on my left foot and heard the sickening sound of a bone cracking, just an instant before the pain hit me.

I lay still, bright red sparks fading from my vision while the pain amped up and up. Trying to think, not scream.

My ankle was probably broken, and at least one rib on the left side. I breathed deeply, listening—Paul told me about how he had broken a rib in a car wreck, and he could tell by the sound that it had punctured his lung. This did hurt, but didn't sound different—and then I realized I was lucky to be breathing at all. The helmet and suit were intact.

But would I be able to keep breathing long enough to be rescued?

The suit light was out. I clicked the switch over and over, and nothing happened. If I could find the dog, and if it was intact, I'd have an extra sixteen hours of oxygen. Otherwise, I probably had two, two and a half hours.

I didn't suppose the radio would do any good, underground, but I tried it anyway. Yelled into it for a minute and then listened. Nothing.

These suits ought to have some sort of beeper to trace people with. But then I guess nobody else ever wandered off and disappeared.

It was about four. How long before someone woke up and noticed I was gone? How long before someone got worried enough to check, and see that the suit and dog were missing?

I tried to stand and it wasn't possible. The pain was intolerable and the bone made an ominous sound. I couldn't help crying but stopped after a minute. Pathetic.

Had to find the dog, with its oxygen and power. I stretched out and patted the ground back and forth, and scrabbled around in a circle, feeling for it.

It wasn't anywhere nearby. But how far could it have rolled after it hit?

I had to be careful, not just crawl off in some random direction and get lost. I remembered feeling a large, kind of pointy, rock off to my left—good thing I hadn't landed on it—and could use it as a reference point.

I found it and moved up so my feet were touching it. Visualizing an old-fashioned clock with me as the hour hand, I went off in the 12:00 direction, measuring four body lengths inchworm style. Then crawled back to the pointy rock and did the same thing in the opposite, 6:00, direction. Nothing there, nor at 9:00 or 3:00, and I tried not to panic.

In my mind's eye I could see the areas where I hadn't been able to reach, the angles midway between 12:00 and 3:00, 3:00 and 6:00, and so on. I went back to the pointy rock and started over. On the second try, my hand touched one of the dog's wheels, and I smiled in spite of my situation.

It was lying on its side. I uprighted it and felt for the switch that would turn on its light. When it came on, I was looking straight into it and it dazzled me blind.

Facing away from it, after a couple of minutes I could see some of where I was. I'd fallen into a large underground cavern, maybe shaped like a dome, though I couldn't see as far as the top. I guessed it was part of a lava tube that was almost open to the surface, worn so thin that it couldn't support my weight.

Maybe it joined up with the lava tube that we lived in! But even if it did, and even if I knew which direction to go, I couldn't crawl the four kilometers back. I tried to ignore the pain and do the math, anyhow—sixteen hours of oxygen, four kilometers, that means creeping 250 meters per hour, dragging the dog along behind me...no way. Better to hope they would track me down here.

What were the chances of that? Maybe the dog's tracks, or my boot prints? Only in dusty places, if the wind didn't cover them up before dawn.

If they searched at night, the dog's light might help. How close would a person have to come to the hole, to see it? Close enough to crash through and join me?

And would the dog's power supply last long enough to shine all night and again tomorrow night? It wouldn't have to last any longer than that.

The ankle was hurting less, but that was because of numbness. My hands and feet were getting cold. Was that a suit malfunction, or just because I was stretched out on this cold cave floor. Where the sun had never shined.

With a start, I realized the coldness could mean that my suit was losing power—it should automatically warm up the gloves and boots. I opened my mouth wide and with my chin pressed the switch that ought to project a technical readout in front of my eyes, with "power remaining," and nothing came up.

Well, the dog obviously had power to spare. I unreeled the recharge cable and plugged its jack into my LSU.

Nothing happened.

I chinned the switch over and over. Nothing.

Maybe it was just the readout display that was broken; I was getting power but it wasn't registering. Trying not to panic, I wiggled the jack, unplugged and replugged it. Still nothing.

I was breathing, though; that part worked. I unrolled the umbilical hose from the dog and pushed the fitting into the bottom of the LSU. It made a loud pop and a sudden breeze of cold oxygen blew around my neck and chin.

So at least I wouldn't die of that. I would be frozen solid before I ran out of air; how comforting. Acid rush of panic in my throat; I choked it back and sucked on the water tube until the nausea was gone.

Which made me think about the other end, and I clamped up. I was not going to fill the suit's emergency diaper with shit and piss before I died. Though the people who deal with dead people probably have seen that before. And it would be frozen solid, so what's the difference. Inside the body or outside.

I stopped crying long enough to turn on the radio and say goodbye to people, and apologize for my stupidity. Though it's unlikely that anyone would ever hear it. Unless there was some kind of secret recorder in the suit, thanks to the Dragon, and someone stumbled on it years from now.

I wished I had Dad's zen. If Dad were in this situation he would just accept it, and wait to leave his body.

I tipped the dog up on end, so its light shone directly up toward the hole I'd fallen through, still too high up to see.

I couldn't feel my feet or hands anymore and was growing heavy-lidded. I'd read that freezing to death was the least painful way to go, and one of my last coherent thoughts was "Who came back to tell them?"

Then I hallucinated an angel, wearing red, surrounded by an ethereal bubble. He was incredibly ugly.

6. ANGEL IN HELL

I woke up in some pain, ankle throbbing and hands and feet burning. I was lying on a huge inflated pillow. The air was thick and muggy and it was dark. A yellow light was bobbing toward me, growing brighter. I heard lots of feet.

It was a flashlight, or rather a lightstick like you wear night-dancing, and the person holding it…wasn't a person. It was the red angel from my dream.

Maybe I was still dreaming. I was naked, which sometimes happens in my dreams. The dog was sitting a few feet away. My broken ankle was splinted between two pieces of what felt like wood. On Mars?

This angel had too many legs, like four, sticking out from under the red tunic thing. His head, if that's what it was, looked like a potato that had gone really bad. Soft and wrinkled and covered with eyes. Maybe they *were* eyes, lots of them, or antennae. Like fat hairs that moved around. He was almost as big as a small horse. He seemed to have two regular-sized arms and two little ones. For an angel, he smelled a lot like tuna fish.

I should have been terrified, naked in front of this monster, but he definitely was the one who had saved me from freezing to death. Or he was dressed like that one.

"Are you real?" I said. "Or am I still dreaming, or dead?"

He made some kind of noise, sort of like a bullfrog with teeth chattering. Then he whistled and the lights came on, dim but enough to see around. The unreality of it made me dizzy.

I was taking it far too calmly, maybe because I couldn't think of a thing to do. Either I was in the middle of some complicated dream, or this is what happens to you after you die, or I was completely insane, or, least likely of all, I'd been rescued by a Martian.

But a Martian wouldn't breathe oxygen, not this thick. He wouldn't have wood for making splints. Though this one might know something about ankles, having so many of them.

"You don't speak English, do you?"

He responded with a long speech that sounded kind of threatening. Maybe it was about food animals not being allowed to talk.

I was in a circular room, a little too small for both me and Big Red, with a round wall that seemed to be several layers of plastic sheeting. He had come in through slits in the plastic. The polished stone floor was warm. The high ceiling looked like the floor, but there were four bluish lights imbedded in it, that looked like cheap plastic decorations.

It felt like a hospital room, and maybe it was one. The pillow was big enough for one like him to lie down on it.

On a stone pedestal over by the dog was a pitcher and a glass made of something that looked like obsidian. He poured me a glass of something and brought it over.

His hand, also potato-brown, had four long fingers without nails, and lots of little joints. The fingers were all the same length and it looked like any one of them could be the thumb. The small hands were miniature versions of the big ones.

The stuff in the glass didn't smell like anything and tasted like water, so I drank it down in a couple of greedy gulps.

He took the glass back and refilled it. When he handed it to me, he pointed into it with a small hand, and said, "Ar." Sort of like a pirate.

I pointed and said, "Water?" He answered with a sound like "war," with a lot of extra R's.

He set down the glass and brought me a plate with something that looked remarkably like a mushroom. No, thanks. I read that story.

(For a mad moment I wondered whether that could be it—I *had* eaten, or ingested, something that caused all this, and it was one big dope dream. But the pain was too real.)

He picked the thing up delicately and a mouth opened up in his neck, broad black teeth set in grisly red. He took a small nibble and replaced it on the plate. I shook my head no, though that could mean yes in Martian. Or some mortal insult.

How long could I go without eating? A week, I supposed, but my stomach growled at the thought.

He heard the growling and pointed helpfully to a hole in the floor. That took care of one question, but not quite yet, pal. We've hardly been introduced, and I don't even let my *brother* watch me do that.

I touched my chest and said "Carmen." Then I pointed at his chest, if that's what it was.

He touched his chest and said "Harn." Well, that was a start.

"No." I took his hand—dry, raspy skin—and brought it over to touch my chest. "Car-men," I said slowly. Me Jane, you Tarzan. Or Mr. Potato Head.

"Harn," he repeated, which wasn't a bad Carmen if you couldn't pronounce C or M. Then he took my hand gently and placed it between his two small arms and made a sputtering sound no human could do, at least with the mouth. He let go but I kept my hand there and said, "Red. I'll call you Red."

"Reh," he said, and repeated it. It gave me a shiver. I was communicating with an alien. Someone put up a plaque! But he turned abruptly and left.

I took advantage of being alone and hopped over to the hole and used it, not as easy as that sounds. I needed to find something to use as a crutch. This wasn't exactly Wal-Mart, though. I drank some water and hopped back to the pillow and flopped down.

My hands and feet hurt a little less. They were red, like bad sunburn, which I supposed was the first stage of frostbite. I could have lost some fingers and toes—not that it would matter much to me, with lungs full of ice.

I looked around. Was I inside of Mars or was this some kind of a space ship? You wouldn't make a space ship out of stone. We had to be underground, but this stone didn't look at all like the petrified lava of the colony's tunnel. And it was warm, which had to be electrical or something. The lights and plastic sheets looked pretty high-tech, but everything else was kind of basic—a hole in the floor? (I hoped it wasn't somebody else's ceiling!)

I mentally reviewed why there can't be higher forms of life on Mars, least of all technological life: No artifacts—we've mapped every inch of it, and anything that looked artificial turned out to be natural. Of course there's nothing to breathe, though I seemed to be breathing. Same thing with water. And temperature.

There are plenty of microscopic organisms living underground, but how could they evolve into big bozos like Red? What is there on Mars for a big animal to eat? Rocks?

Red was coming back with his lightstick, followed by someone only half his size, wearing bright lime green. Smoother skin, like a more fresh potato. I decided she was female and called her Green. Just for the time being; I might have it backward. They had seen me naked, but I hadn't seen them—and wasn't eager to, actually. They were scary enough this way.

Green was carrying a plastic bag with things inside that clicked softly together. She set the bag down carefully and exchanged a few noises with Red.

First she took out a dish that looked like pottery, and from a plastic bag shook out something that looked like an herb, or pot. It started smoking immediately, and she thrust it toward me. I sniffed it; it was pleasant, like mint or menthol. She made a gesture with her two small hands, a kind of shooing motion, that I interpreted to mean "breathe more deeply," and I did.

She took the dish away and brought two transparent disks, like big lenses, out of the bag and handed one to me. While I held it, she pressed the other one against my forehead, then chest, then the side of my leg. She gently lifted up the foot with the broken ankle, and pressed it against the sole. Then she did the other foot. She put the lenses back in her bag and stood motionless, staring at me like a doctor or scientist.

I thought, okay, this is where the alien sticks a tube up your ass, but she must have left her tube back at the office.

She and Red conferred for a while, making gestures with their small arms while they made noises like porpoises and machinery. Then she reached into the bag and pulled out a small metal tube, which caused me to cringe away, but she gave it a snap with her wrist and it ratcheted out to about six feet long. She mimicked using it as a cane, which looked really strange, like a spider missing four legs, and handed it to me, saying "Harn."

Guess that was my name now. The stick felt lighter than aluminum, but when I used it to lever myself up, it was rigid and strong.

She reached into her bag of tricks and brought out a thing like her tunic, somewhat thicker and softer and colored gray. There was a hole in it for my head, but no sleeves or other complications. I put it on gratefully and draped it around so I could use the stick. It was agreeably warm.

Red stepped ahead and, with a rippling gesture of all four hands, indicated "Follow me." I did, with Green coming behind me.

It was a strange sensation, going through the slits in those plastic sheets, or whatever they were. It was like they were alive, millions of feathery fingers clasping you and then letting go all at once, to close behind you with a snap.

When I went through the first one, it was noticeably cooler, and cooler still after the second one, and my ears popped. After the fourth one, it felt close to freezing, though the floor was still warm, and the air was noticeably thin; I was almost panting, and could see my breath.

We stepped into a huge dark cavern. Rows of dim lights at about knee level marked off paths. The lights were all blue, but each path had its own kind of blue, different in shade or intensity. Meet me at the corner of bright turquoise and dim aquamarine.

I tried to remember our route, left at this shade and then right at *this* one, but I was not sure how useful the knowledge would be. What, I was going to escape? Hold my breath and run back to the base?

We went through a single sheet into a large area, at least as well lit as my hospital room, and almost as warm. It had a kind of barnyard smell, not unpleasant. There were things that had to be plants all around, like broccoli but brown and gray with some yellow, sitting in water that you could hear was flowing. A little mist hung near the ground, and my face felt damp. It was a hydroponic farm like ours, but without greens or the bright colors of tomatoes and peppers and citrus fruits.

Green leaned over and picked something that looked like a cigar, or something less polite, and offered it to me. I waved it away; she broke it in two and gave half to Red.

I couldn't tell how big the place was, probably acres. So where were all the people it was set up to feed?

I got a partial answer when we passed through another sheet, into a brighter room about the size of the new pod we'd brought on the *John Carter*. There were about twenty of the aliens arranged along two walls, standing at tables or in front of things like data screens, but made of metal rather than plastic. There weren't any chairs; I supposed quadrupeds don't need them.

They all began to move toward me, making strange noises, of course. If I'd brought one of them into a room, humans would have done the same thing, but nevertheless I felt frightened and helpless. When I shrank back, Red put a protective arm in front of me and said a couple of bullfrog syllables. They all stopped about ten feet away.

Green talked to them more softly, gesturing toward me. Then they stepped forward in an orderly way, by colors—two in tan, three in green, two in blue, and so forth—each standing quietly in front of me for a few seconds. I wondered if the color signified rank. None of the others wore red, and none were as big as Big Red. Maybe he was the alpha male, or the only female, like bees.

What were they doing? Just getting a closer look, or taking turns trying to destroy me with thought waves?

After that presentation, Red gestured for me to come over and look at the largest metal screen.

Interesting. It was a panorama of our greenhouse and the other parts of the colony that were above ground. The picture might have been from the top of Telegraph Hill. Just as I noticed that there were a lot of people standing around—too many for a normal work party—the *John Carter* came sliding into view, a rooster tail of red dust fountaining out behind her. A lot of the people jumped up and down and waved.

Then the screen went black for a few seconds, and a green rectangle opened slowly…it was the airlock light at night, as the door slid open. I was looking at myself, just a little while ago, coming out and pulling the dog behind me.

The camera must have been like those flying bugs that Homeland Security spies use. I certainly hadn't seen anything.

When the door closed, the picture changed to a ghostly blue, like moonlight on Earth. It followed me for a minute or so. Stumbling and then staring at the ground as I walked more cautiously.

Then it switched to another location, and I knew what was coming. The ground collapsed and the dog and I disappeared in a cloud of dust, which the wind swept away in an instant.

The bug, or whatever it was, drifted down through the hole to hover over me as I writhed around in pain. A row of glowing symbols appeared at the bottom of the screen. There was a burst of white light when I found the dog and switched it on.

Then Big Red floated down—this was obviously the speeded-up version—wearing several layers of that wall plastic, it seemed; riding a thing that looked like a metal sawhorse with two sidecars. He put me in one and the dog in the other. Then he floated back up.

Then they skipped all the way to me lying on that pillow, naked and unlovely, in an embarrassing posture—I blushed, as if any of them cared—and then moved in close to my ankle, which was blue and swollen. Then a solid holo of a human skeleton, obviously mine, in the same position. The image moved in the same way as before. The fracture line glowed red, and then my foot, below the break, shifted slightly. The line glowed blue and disappeared.

Just then I noticed it wasn't hurting anymore.

Green stepped over and gently took the staff away from me. I put weight on the foot and it felt as good as new.

"How could you do that?" I said, not expecting an answer.

No matter how good they were at healing themselves, how could they apply that to a human skeleton?

Well, a human vet could treat a broken bone in an animal she'd never seen before. But it wouldn't heal in a matter of hours.

Two of the amber ones brought out my skinsuit and Mars suit, and put them at my feet.

Red pointed at me and then tapped on the screen, which again showed the surface parts of the colony. You could hardly see them for the dust, though; there was a strong storm blowing.

He made an up-and-down gesture with his small arms, and then his large ones, obviously meaning "Get dressed."

So with about a million potato eyes watching, I took off the tunic and got into the skinsuit. The diaper was missing, which made it feel kind of baggy. They must have thrown it away—or analyzed it, ugh.

The creatures stared in silence while I zipped that up and then climbed and wiggled into the Mars suit. I secured the boots and gloves and then clamped the helmet into place, and automatically chinned the switch for an oxygen and power readout, but of course it was still broken. I guess that would be asking too much—"you fixed my ankle but you can't fix a foogly space suit? What kind of Martians *are* you?"

It was obvious I wasn't getting any air from the backpack, though. I'd need the dog's backup supply.

I unshipped the helmet and faced Green, and made an exaggerated pantomime of breathing in and out. She didn't react. Hell, they probably breathed by osmosis or something.

I turned to Red and crouched over, patting the air at the level of the dog. "Dog," I said, and pointed back the way we'd come.

He leaned over and mimicked my gesture, and said, "Nog." Pretty close. Then he turned to the crowd and croaked out a speech, which I think had both "Harn" and "nog" in it.

He must have understood, at least partly, because he made that four-armed "come along" motion at me, and went back to the place where we'd entered. I went through the plastic and looked back. Green was leading four others, it looked like one of each color, following us.

Red leading us, we all went back along what seemed the same path we'd used coming over. I counted my steps, so that when I told people about it I'd have at least one actual concrete number. The hydroponic room, or at least the part we cut through, was 185 steps wide; then it was another 204 steps from there to the "hospital" room. I get about 80 centimeters to a step, so the trip covered more than 300 meters, allowing for a little dog-leg in the middle. Of course it might go on for miles in every direction, but at least it was no smaller than that.

We went into the little room and they watched while I unreeled the umbilical and plugged it in. The cool air coming through the neck fitting was more than a relief. I put my helmet back on. Green stepped forward and did a pretty good imitation of my breathing pantomime.

I sort of didn't want to go. I was looking forward to coming back, and learning how to communicate with Red and Green. We had other people more qualified, though. I should have listened to Mother when she got after me to take a language in school. If I'd known this was going to happen, I would have taken Chinese and Latin and Body Noises.

The others stood away from the plastic and Red gestured for me to follow. I pulled the dog along through the four plastic layers; this time we turned sharply to the right and started walking up a gently sloping ramp.

After a few minutes I could look down and get a sense of how large this place was. There was the edge of a lake—an immense amount of water even if it was only a few inches deep. From above, the buildings looked like domes of clay, or just dirt, with no windows, just the pale blue light that filtered through the door layers.

There were squares of different sizes and shades that were probably crops like the mushrooms and cigars, and one large square had trees that looked like six-foot-tall broccoli, which could explain the wooden splints.

We came to a level place, brightly lit, that had shelves full of bundles of the plastic stuff. Red walked straight to one shelf and pulled off a bundle. It was his Mars suit. Bending over at a strange angle, bobbing, he slid his feet into four opaque things like thick socks. His two large arms went into sleeves, ending in mittens. Then the whole thing seemed to come alive, and ripple up and over him, sealing together and then inflating. It didn't have anything that looked like an oxygen tank, but air was coming from somewhere.

He gestured for me to follow and we went toward a dark corner. He hesitated there, and held out his hand to me. I took it, and we staggered slowly through dozens of layers of the stuff, toward a dim light.

It was obviously like a gradual airlock. We stopped at another flat area, which had one of the blue lights, and rested for a few minutes. Then he led me through another long series of layers, where it became completely dark—without him leading me, I might have gotten turned around—and then it lightened slightly, the light pink this time.

When we came out, we were on the floor of a cave; the light was coming from a circle of Martian sky. When my eyes adjusted, I could see there was a smooth ramp leading uphill to the cave entrance.

I'd never seen the sky that color. We were looking up through a serious dust storm.

Red pulled a dust-covered sheet off his sawhorse-shaped vehicle. I helped him put the dog into one of the bowl-like sidecars, and I got in the other. There were two things like stubby handlebars in front, but no other controls that I could see.

He backed onto the thing, straddling it, and we rose off the ground a foot or so, and smoothly started forward.

The glide up the ramp was smooth. I expected to be buffeted around by the dust storm, but as impressive as it looked, it didn't have much power. My umbilical tube did flap around in the wind, which made me nervous. If it snapped, a failsafe would close off the tube so I wouldn't immediately die. But I'd use up the air in the suit pretty fast.

I couldn't see more than ten or twenty feet in any direction, but Red, I hoped, could see farther. He was moving very fast. Of course, he was unlikely to hit another vehicle, or a tree.

I settled down into the bowl—there wasn't anything to see—and was fairly comfortable. I amused myself by imagining the reaction of Dargo Solingen and Mother and Dad when I showed up with an actual Martian.

It felt like an hour or more before he slowed down and we hit the ground and skidded to a stop. He got off his perch laboriously and came around to the dog's side. I got out to help him lift it and was knocked off balance by a gust. Four legs were a definite advantage here.

He watched while I got the umbilical untangled and then pointed me in the direction we were headed. Then he made a shooing motion.

"You have to come with me," I said, uselessly, and tried to translate it into arm motions. He pointed and shooed again, and then backed on to the sawhorse and took off in a slow U-turn.

I started to panic. What if I went in the wrong direction? I could miss the base by twenty feet and just keep walking on into the desert.

I took a few deep breaths. The dog was pointed in the right direction. I picked up its handle and looked straight ahead as far as I could see, through the swirling gloom. I saw a rock, directly ahead, and walked to it. Then another rock, maybe ten feet away. After the fourth rock, I looked up and saw I'd almost run into the airlock door. I leaned on the big red button and the door slid open immediately. It closed behind the dog and the red light on the ceiling started blinking. It turned green and the inside door opened on a wide-eyed Emily.

"Carmen! You found your way back!"

"Well, um…not really…"

"Got to call the search party!" She bounded down the stairs yelling for Howard.

I wondered how long they'd been searching for me. I would be in shit up to my chin.

I put the dog back in its place—there was only one other parked there, so three were out looking for me. Or my body.

Card came running in when I was half out of my skinsuit. "Sis!" He grabbed me and hugged me, which was moderately embarrassing. "We thought you were—"

"Yeah, okay. Let me get dressed? Before the shit hits the fan?" He let me turn around and step out of the skinsuit and into my coverall.

"What, you went out for a walk and got lost in that dust storm?"

For a long moment, I thought of saying yes. Who was going to believe my story? I looked at the clock and saw that it was 1900. If it was the same day, seventeen hours had passed. I *could* have wandered around that long without running out of air.

"How long have I been gone?"

"You can't remember? All foogly day, man. Were you derilious?"

"Delirious." I kneaded my brow and rubbed my face hard with both hands. "Let me wait and tell it all when Mother and Dad get here."

"That'll be hours! They're out looking for you."

"Oh, that's great. Who else?"

"I think it was Paul the pilot."

"Well," said a voice behind me. "You decided to come back after all."

It was Dargo Solingen. There was a quaver of emotion in her voice that I'd never heard. I think anger.

"I'm sorry," I said. "I don't know what I was thinking."

"I don't think you were thinking at *all.* You were being a foolish *girl,* and you put more lives than your own into danger."

About a dozen people were behind her. "Dargo," Dr. Jefferson said. "She's back, she's alive. Let's give her a little rest."

"Has she given *us* any rest?" she barked.

"I'm *sorry!* I'll do anything—"

"You will? Isn't that pretty. What do you propose to do?"

Dr. Estrada put a hand on her shoulder. "Please let me talk to her." Oh, good, a shrink. I needed a xenologist. But she would listen better than Solingen.

"Oh...do what you want. I'll deal with her later." She turned and walked through the small crowd.

Some people gathered around me and I tried not to cry. I wouldn't want *her* to think she had made me cry. But there were plenty of shoulders and arms for me to hide my eyes in.

"Carmen." Dr. Estrada touched my forearm. "We ought to talk before your parents get back."

"Okay." A dress rehearsal. I followed her down to the middle of A.

She had a large room to herself, but it was her office as well as quarters. "Lie down here," she indicated her single bunk, "and just try to relax. Begin at the beginning."

"The beginning isn't very interesting. Dargo Solingen embarrassed me in front of everybody. Not the first time, either. Sometimes I feel like I'm her little project. Let's drive Carmen crazy."

"So in going outside like that, you were getting back at her? Getting even in some way?"

"I didn't think of it that way. I just had to get out, and that was the only way."

"Maybe not, Carmen. We can work on ways to get away without physically leaving."

"Like Dad's zen thing, okay. But what I did, or why, isn't really important. It's what I *found!*"

"So what did you find?"

"Life. Intelligent life. They saved me." I could hear my voice and even I didn't believe it.

"Hmm," she said. "Go on."

"I'd walked four kilometers or so and was about to turn around and go back. But I stepped on a place that wouldn't support my weight. Me and the dog. We fell through. At least ten meters, maybe twenty."

"And you weren't hurt?"

"I *was!* I heard my ankle break. I broke a rib, maybe more than one, here."

She pressed the area, gently. "But you're walking."

"They fixed…I'm getting ahead of myself."

"So you fell through and broke your ankle?"

"Then I spent a long time finding the dog. My suit light went out when I hit the ground. But finally I found it, found the dog, and got my umbilical plugged in."

"So you had plenty of oxygen."

"But I was freezing. The circuit to my gloves and boots wasn't working. I really thought that was it."

"But you survived."

"I was rescued. I was passing out and this, uh, this *Martian* came floating down, I saw him in the dog's light. Then everything went black and I woke up—"

"Carmen! You have to see that this was a dream. A hallucination."

"Then how did I get here?"

Her mouth set in a stubborn line. "You were very lucky. You wandered around in the storm and came back here."

"But there *was* no storm when I left! Just a little wind. The storm came up while I was…well, I was underground. Where the Martians live."

"You've been through so much, Carmen…"

"This was *not* a dream!" I tried to stay calm. "Look. You can check the air left in the tanks. My suit and the dog. There will be *hours* unaccounted for. I was breathing the Martians' air."

"Carmen…be reasonable…"

"No, *you* be reasonable. I'm not saying anything more until—" There was one knock on the door and Mother burst in, followed by Dad.

"My baby," she said. When did she ever call me that? She hugged me so hard I could barely breathe. "You found your way back."

"Mother…I was just telling Dr. Estrada…I didn't find my way back. I was brought."

"She had a dream about Martians. A hallucination."

"*No!* Would you just listen?"

Dad sat down cross-legged, looking up at me. "Start at the beginning, honey."

I did. I took a deep breath and started with taking the suit and the dog and going out to be alone. Falling and breaking my ankle. Waking up in the little hospital room. Red and Green and the others. Seeing the base on their screen. Being healed and brought back.

There was an uncomfortable silence after I finished. "If it wasn't for the dust storm," Dad said, "it would be easy to verify your...your account. Nobody could see you from here, though, and the satellites won't show anything, either."

"Maybe that's why he was in a rush to bring me back. If they'd waited for the storm to clear, they'd be exposed."

"Why would they be afraid of that?" Dr. Estrada asked.

"Well, I don't know. But I guess it's obvious that they don't want anything to do with us—"

"Except to rescue a lost girl," Mother said.

"Is that so hard to believe? I mean, I couldn't say three words to them, but I could tell they were good-hearted."

"It just sounds so fantastic," Dad said. "How would you feel in our position? By far the easiest explanation is that you were under extreme stress and—"

"*No!* Dad, do you really think I would do that? Come up with some elaborate lie?" I could see on his face that he did indeed. Maybe not a lie, but a fantasy. "There's objective proof. Look at the dog. It has a huge dent where it hit the ground in the cave."

"Maybe so; I haven't seen it," he said. "But being devil's advocate, aren't there many other ways that could have happened?"

"What about the *air!* The air in the dog! I didn't use enough of it to have been out so long."

He nodded. "That would be compelling. Did you dock it?"

Oh hell. "Yes. I wasn't thinking I'd have to *prove* anything." When you dock the dog it automatically starts to refill air and power. "There must be a record. How much oxygen a dog takes on when it recharges."

They all looked at each other. "Not that I know of," Dad said. "But you don't need that. Let's just do an MRI of your ankle. That'll tell if it was recently broken."

"But they *fixed* it. The break might not show."

"It will show," Dr. Estrada said. "Unless there was some kind of…magic involved."

Mother's face was getting red. "Would you both leave? I need to talk to Carmen alone." They both nodded and went out.

Mother watched the door close. "I know you aren't lying. You've never been good at that."

"Thanks," I said. Thanks for nothing.

"But it was a stupid thing to do, going off like that, and you know it."

"I do, I *do!* And I'm sorry for all the trouble I—"

"But look. I'm a scientist, and so is your dad, after a fashion, and so is almost everybody else who's going to hear this story today. You see what I'm saying?"

"Yeah, I think so. They're going to be skeptical."

"Of course they are. They don't get paid for believing things. They get paid for questioning them."

"And you, Mother. Do you believe me?"

She stared at me with a fierce intensity I'd never seen before in my life. "Look. Whatever happened to you, I believe one hundred percent that you're telling the truth. You're telling the truth about what you remember, what you believe happened."

"But I might be nuts."

"Well, wouldn't you say so? If I came in with your story? You'd say 'Mom's getting old.' Wouldn't you?"

"Yeah, maybe I would."

"And to prove that I wasn't crazy, I would take you out and show you something that couldn't be explained any other way. You know what they say about extraordinary claims?"

"They require extraordinary evidence."

"That's right. Once the storm calms down, you and I are going out to where you say...to where you fell through to the cave." She put her hand on the back of my head and rubbed my hair. "I so much want to believe you. For my sake as well as yours. To find life here."

7. THE DRAGON LADY

Mother wanted to call a general assembly, so I could tell everybody the complete story, all at once, but Dargo Solingen wouldn't allow it. She said that children do stunts like this to draw attention to themselves, and she wasn't going to reward me with an audience. Of course she's an expert about children, never having had any herself. Good thing. They'd be monsters.

So it was like the whisper game, where you sit in a circle and whisper a sentence to the person next to you, and she whispers it to the next, and so on. When it gets back to you, it's all wrong, sometimes in a funny way.

This was not particularly funny. People would ask if I was really going around on the surface without a Mars suit, or think the Martians stripped me naked and interrogated me, or they broke my ankle on purpose. I put a detailed account on my website, but a lot of people would rather talk than read.

The MRI didn't help much, except for people who wanted to believe I was lying. Dr. Jefferson said it looked like an old childhood injury, long ago healed. Mother was with me at the time, and she told him she was absolutely sure I'd never broken that ankle. To people like Dargo Solingen that was a big shrug; so I'd lied about that, too. I think we won Dr. Jefferson over, though he was inclined to believe me, anyhow. So did most of the people who came over on the *John Carter* with us. They were willing to believe in Martians before they'd believe I would make up something like that.

Dad didn't want to talk about it, but Mother was fascinated. I went to talk with her at the lab after dinner (she and two others were keeping a 24-hour watch on an experiment). "I don't see how they could be actual Martians," she said, "in the sense that we're Earthlings. I mean, if they evolved here as oxygen-water creatures similar to us, then that was three billion years ago. And, as you said, a large animal isn't going to evolve alone, without any other animals. Nor will it suddenly appear, without smaller, simpler animals preceding it. So they must be like us."

"From Earth?"

She laughed. "I don't think so. None of the eight-limbed creatures on Earth has very high technology. I think they have to have come from yet another planet. Unless we're completely wrong about areology, about the history of conditions on this planet, they can't have come from here."

"What if they used to live on the surface?" I said. "Then moved underground as the planet dried up and lost its air?"

She shook her head. "The time scale. No species more complicated than a bacterium has survived for billions of years."

"None on Earth," I said.

"Touché," she laughed. A bell chimed and she went to the other side of the room and looked inside an aquarium, or terrarium. Or ares-arium, here, I suppose. She looked at the things growing inside and typed some numbers onto her clipboard.

"So they went underground three billion years ago with the technology to duplicate what sounds like a high-altitude Earth environment. And stayed that way for three billion years." She shook her head. "It's not likely. And I still want to know where the fossils are. Maybe they dug them all up and destroyed them, just to confuse us?"

"But it's not like we've looked everywhere. Paul says it may be that life wasn't distributed uniformly, and we just haven't found any of the islands where things lived. The dinosaurs or whatever."

"Well, you know it didn't work that way on Earth. Fossils everywhere, from the bottom of the sea to the top of the Himalayas. Crocodile fossils in Antarctica."

"Okay. That's Earth."

"It's all we have. Coffee?" I said no and she poured herself half a cup. "You're right that it's weak to generalize from one example. Paul could very well be right, too; there's no evidence one way or the other.

"But look. We know all about one form of life on Mars: you and me and the others. We have to live in an artificial bubble that contains an alien environment, maintained by high technology, because we *are* the aliens here. So you stumble on eight-legged potato people who also live in a bubble that contains an alien environment, evidently maintained by high technology. The simplest explanation is that they're aliens, too. Alien to Mars."

"Yeah, I don't disagree. I know about Occam's Razor."

She smiled at that. "What's fascinating to me, one of many things, is that you spent hours in that environment and felt no ill effects. Their planet's very earthlike."

"What if it *was* Earth?"

That stopped her. "Wouldn't we have noticed?"

"I mean a long time ago. What if they lived only on mountain tops, and developed high technology thousands and thousands of years ago. Then they all left."

"It's an idea," she said. "But it's hard to believe that every one of them would be willing and able to leave—and that there would be no trace of their civilization, ten or even a hundred thousand years later. And where are their genetic precursors? The eight-legged equivalent of apes?"

"You don't really believe me."

"Well, I do; I do," she said seriously. "I just don't think there's an easy explanation."

"Like Dargo Solingen's? The Figment of Imagination Theory?"

"Especially that. People don't have complex consistent hallucinations; they're *called* hallucinations because they're fantastic, dreamlike.

"Besides, I saw the dog; you couldn't have put that dent in it with a lead-lined baseball bat. And she can't explain the damage to your Mars suit, either, without positing that you leaped off the side of a cliff just to give yourself an alibi." She was getting worked up. "And I'm your *mother*, even if I'm not a model one. I would goddamn remember if you had ever broken your ankle! That healed hairline fracture is enough proof for me—and for Dr. Jefferson and Dr. Milius and anybody else in this goddamned hole who didn't convict you before you opened your mouth."

"You've been a good mother," I said.

She suddenly sat up and hugged me across the table. "Not so good. Or you wouldn't have done this."

She sat down and rubbed my hand. "But if you hadn't done it—" She laughed. "—how long would it have been before we stumbled on these aliens? They're watching us, but don't seem eager to have us see them."

The window on the wall was a greenboard of differential equations. She clicked on her clipboard and it became a real-time window. The storm was still blowing, but it had thinned out enough so I could see a vague outline of Telegraph Hill.

"Maybe tomorrow we'll be able to go out and take a look. If Paul's free, he'd probably like to come along; nobody knows the local real estate better than him."

I stood up. "I can hardly wait. But I *will* wait, promise."

"Good. Once is enough." She smiled up at me. "Get some rest. Probably a long day tomorrow."

Actually, I was up past midnight catching up on schoolwork, or not quite catching up. My brain wouldn't settle down enough to worry about Kant and his Categorical Imperative. Not with aliens out there waiting to be contacted.

8. BAD COUGH

Paul was free until 1400, so right after breakfast we suited up and equipped a dog with extra oxygen and climbing gear. He'd done a lot of climbing and caving on both Earth and Mars. If we found the hole—*when* we found the hole— he was going to approach it roped up, so if he broke through the way I did, he wouldn't fall far or fast.

I'd awakened early with a slight cough, but felt okay. I got some cough suppressant pills from the first-aid locker, chewed one and put two in my helmet's tongue-operated pill cache.

We went through the airlock and weren't surprised to see that the storm had covered all my tracks, and everyone else's— including Red's; I was hoping that his sawhorse thing might have gouged out a distinctive mark when it stopped.

We still had a good chance of finding the hole, thanks to the MPS built into the suit and its inertial compass. I'd started counting steps, going west, when I set out from Telegraph Hill, and was close to five thousand when I fell through. That's about four kilometers, maybe an hour's walk in the daytime.

"So we're probably being watched," Mother said, and waved to the invisible camera. "Hey there, Mr. Red! Hello, Dr. Green! We're bringing back your patient with the insurance forms."

I waved, too, both arms. Paul put up both his hands palm out, showing he wasn't armed. Though what it would mean to a four-armed creature, I wasn't sure.

No welcoming party appeared, so we went to the right of Telegraph Hill and started walking and counting. A lot of the terrain looked familiar. Several times I had us move to the left or right when I was sure I had been closer to a given formation.

We walked a half-kilometer or so past Paul's wrecked dumbo. I hadn't seen it in the dark.

Suddenly I noticed something. "Wait! Paul! I think it's just ahead of you." I hadn't realized it, walking in the dark, but what seemed to be a simple rise in the ground was actually rounded, like an overturned shallow bowl.

"Like a little lava dome, maybe," he said. "That's where you fell through." He pointed at something I couldn't quite see from my angle and height. "Big enough for you and the dog, anyhow."

He unloaded his mountaineering stuff from the dog, then took a hammer and pounded into the ground a long piton, which is like a spearpoint with a hole for the rope. Then he did another one about a foot away. He passed an end of the rope through both of them and tied it off.

He pulled on the rope with all his weight. "Carmen, Laura, help me test this." We did and it still held. He looped most of the rope over his shoulder and took a couple of turns under his arms, and then clamped it through a metal thing he called a crab. It's supposed to keep you from falling too fast, even if you let go.

"This probably isn't all necessary," he said, "since I'm just taking a look down. But better safe than dead." He backed up the slight incline, checking over his shoulder, and then got on his knees to approach the hole.

I held my breath as he took out a big flashlight and leaned over the edge. I didn't hear mother breathing, either.

"Okay!" he said. "There's the side reflector that broke off your dog. I've got a good picture."

"Good," I tried to say, but it came out as a cough. Then another cough, and then several, harder and harder. I felt faint and sat down and tried to stay calm. Eyes closed, shallow breathing.

When I opened my eyes, I saw specks of blood on the inside of my helmet. I could taste it inside my mouth and on my lips. "Mother, I'm sick."

She saw the blood and kneeled down next to me. "Breathe. Can you breathe?"

"Yes. I don't think it's the suit." She was checking the oxygen fitting and meter on the back.

"How long have you felt sick?"

"Not long…well, *now* I do. I had a little cough this morning."

"And didn't tell anybody."

"No, I took a pill and it was all right."

"I can see how all right it was. Do you think you can stand?"

I nodded and got to my feet, wobbling a little. She held on to my arm. Then Paul came up and held the other.

"I can just see the antenna on Telegraph Hill," he said. "I'll call for the jeep."

"No, don't," I pleaded. "I don't want to give the Dragon the satisfaction."

Mother gave a nervous laugh. "This is way beyond that, sweetheart. Blood in your lungs? What if I let you walk back and you dropped dead?"

"I'm not going to *die*." But saying that gave me a horrible chill. Then I coughed a bright red string onto my faceplate. Mother eased me back down, and awkwardly sat with my helmet in her lap while Paul shouted "Mayday!" over the radio.

"Where did they come up with that word?" I asked Mother.

"Easy to understand on a radio, I guess. 'Mo' dough' would work just as well." I heard the click as her glove touched my helmet. Trying to smooth my hair.

I didn't cry. Embarrassing to admit, but I guess I felt kind of important, dying and all. Dargo Solingen would feel like shit for doubting me. Though the cause-and-effect link there wasn't too clear.

I lay there trying not to cough for maybe twenty minutes before the jeep pulled up, driven by Dad. One big happy family. He and mother lifted me into the back and Paul took over the driving, leaving the dog and his climbing stuff behind.

It was a fast and rough ride back. I got into another coughing spasm and spattered more blood and goop on the faceplate.

Mother and Dad carried me into the airlock like a sack of grain or something, and then were all over each other trying to get me out of the Mars suit. At least they left the skinsuit on while they hurried me through the corridor and mess area to Dr. Jefferson's aid station.

He asked my parents to step outside, set me on the examination table, and stripped off the top of the skinsuit, to listen to my breathing with a stethoscope. He shook his head.

"Carmen, it sure sounds as if you've got something in your lungs. But when I heard you were coming in with this, I looked at the whole-body MRI we took yesterday, and there's nothing there." He clicked on his clipboard and asked the window for my MRI, and there I was in all my transparent glory.

"Better take another one." He pulled the top up over my shoulders. "You don't have to take anything off; just lie down here." The act of lying down made me cough sharply, but I caught it in my palm.

He took a tissue and gently wiped my hand, and looked at the blood. "Damn," he said quietly. "You aren't a smoker. I mean on Earth."

"Just twice. Once tobacco and once pot. Just one time each."

He nodded. "Now take a really deep breath and try to hold it." He took the MRI wand and passed it back and forth over my upper body. "Okay. You can breathe now.

"New picture," he said to the window. Then he was quiet for too long.

"Oh my. What...what could that be?"

I looked, and there were black shapes in both of my lungs, about the size of golf balls. "What is...what are they?"

He shook his head. "Not cancer, not an infection, this fast. Bronchitis wouldn't show up black, anyhow. Better call Earth." He looked at me with concern and something else, maybe puzzlement. "Let's get you into bed in the next room, and I'll give you a sedative. Stop the coughing. And then maybe I'll take a look inside."

"Inside?"

"Brachioscopy, put a little camera down there. You won't feel anything."

In fact, I didn't feel anything until I woke up several hours later.

Mother was sitting by the bed, her hand on my forehead. "My nose...the inside of my nose feels funny."

"That's where the tube went in. The brachioscope."

"Oh, yuck. Did he find anything?"

She hesitated. "It's...not from Earth. They snipped off some of it and took it to the lab. It's not...it doesn't have DNA."

"I've got a Martian disease?"

"Mars, or wherever your potato people are from. Not Earth, anyhow; everything alive on Earth has DNA."

I prodded where it ached, under my ribs. "It's not organic?"

"Well, it is. Carbon, hydrogen, oxygen. Nitrogen, phosphorus, sulfur—it has amino acids and proteins and even something like RNA. But that's as far as it goes."

That sounded bad enough. "So they're going to have to operate? On both of my lungs?"

She made a little noise and I looked up and saw her wiping her eyes. "What is it? Mother?"

"It's not that simple. The little piece they snipped off, it had to go straight into the glove box, the environmental isolation unit. That's the procedure we have for any Martian life we discover, because we don't know what effect it might have on human life. In your case…"

"In my case, it's already attacked a human."

"That's right. And they can't operate on you in the glove box."

"So they're just going to leave it there?"

"No. But Dr. Jefferson can't operate until he can work in a place that's environmentally isolated from the rest of the base. They're working on it now, turning the far end of Unit B into a little self-contained hospital. You'll move in there tomorrow or the next day, and he'll take out the stuff. Two operations."

"Two?"

"The first lung has to be working before he opens the second. On Earth, he could put you on a heart/lung machine, I guess, and work on both. But not here."

I felt suddenly cold and clammy and I must have turned pale. "It's not that bad," Mother said quickly. "He doesn't have to open you up; he'll be working through a small hole in your side. It's called thorascopy. Like when I had my knee operated on, and I was just in and out. And he'll have the best surgeons on Earth looking over his shoulder, advising him."

With a half-hour delay, I thought. What if their advice was "No—don't do *that!*" Oops.

I thought of an old bad joke: Politicians cover their mistakes with money; cooks cover their mistakes with mayonnaise; doctors cover theirs with dirt. I could be the first person ever buried on Mars, what an honor.

"Wait," I said. "Maybe *they* could help."

"The Earth doctors? Sure—"

"No! I mean the aliens."

"Honey, they couldn't—"

"They fixed my ankle just like that, didn't they?"

"Well, evidently they did. But that's sort of a mechanical thing. They wouldn't have to know any internal medicine..."

"But it wasn't medicine at all, not like we know it. Those big lenses, the smoking herbs. It was kind of mumbo-jumbo, but it worked!"

There was one loud rap on the door, and Dr. Jefferson opened it and stepped inside, looking agitated. "Laura, Carmen—things have gone from bad to worse. The Parienza kids started coughing blood; they've got it. So I put my boy through the MRI, and he's got a mass in one of his lungs, too.

"Look, I have to operate on the Parienzas first; they're young and this is hitting them harder..."

"That's okay," I said. By all means, get some practice on someone else first.

"Laura, I want you to assist me in the surgery along with Selene." Dr. Milius. "So far, this is only infecting the children. If it gets into the general population, if *I* get it—"

"Alf! I'm not a surgeon—I'm not even a doctor!"

"If Selene and I get this and die, you are a doctor. You are *the* doctor. You at least know how to use a scalpel."

"Cutting up animals that are already dead!"

"Just...calm down. The machine's not that complicated. It's a standard waldo interface, and you have real-time MRI to show you where you're going."

"Can you hear yourself talking, Alphonzo? I'm just a biologist."

There was a long moment of silence while he looked at her. "Just come and pay attention. You might have to do Carmen."

"All right," Mother said. She looked grim. "Now?"

He nodded. "Selene's preparing them. I'm going to operate on Murray while she watches and assists; then she'll do Roberta while I observe. Maybe an hour and a half each."

"What can I do?" I said.

"Just stay put and try to rest," he said. "We'll get to you in three or four hours. Don't worry…you won't feel anything." Then he and mother were gone.

Won't feel anything? I was already feeling pretty crappy. I get pissed off and go for a walk and bring back the Plague from Outer Space?

I touched the window and said "Window outside." It was almost completely dark, just a faint line of red showing the horizon. The dust storm was over.

The whole plan crystallized then. I guess I'd been thinking of parts of it since I knew I'd be alone for a while.

I just zipped up my skinsuit and walked. The main corridor was almost deserted, people running along on urgent errands. Nobody was thinking of going outside—no one but me.

If the aliens had had a picture of me leaving the base at two in the morning, before, then they probably were watching us all the time. I could signal them. Send a message to Red.

I searched around for pencil to disable the airlock buzzer. Even while I was doing it, I wondered whether I was acting sanely. Was I just trying to escape being operated on? Mother used to say "Do something, even if it's wrong." There didn't seem to be anything else to do other than sit around and watch things go from bad to worse.

If the aliens were watching, I could make Red understand how serious it was. Whether he and Green could do anything, I didn't know. But what else was there? Things were happening too fast.

I didn't run into anyone until I was almost there. Then I nearly collided with Card as he stepped out of the Pod A bathroom.

"What you doing over here?" he said. "I thought you were supposed to be in sick bay."

"No, I'm just—" Of course I started coughing. "Let me by, all right?"

"No! What are you up to?"

"Look, microbe. I don't have time to explain." I pushed by him. "Every second counts."

"You're going outside again! What are you, crazy?"

"Look, look, look—for once in your life, don't be a…" I had a moment of desperate inspiration, and grabbed him by the shoulders. "Card, listen. I need you. You have to trust me."

"What, this is about your crazy Martian story?"

"I can prove it's not crazy, but you have to come help me."

"Help you with what?"

"Just suit up and step outside with me. I think they'll come if I signal them, and they might be able to help us."

He was hesitant. I knew he only half believed me—but at least he did half believe me. "What? What do you want me to do outside?"

"I just want you to stand in the door, so the airlock can't close. That way no grown-up can come out and froog the deal."

That did make him smile. "So what you want is for me to be in as deep shit as you are."

"Exactly! Are you up for it?"

"You are so easy to see through, you know? You could be a window."

"Yeah, yeah. Are you with me?"

He glanced toward the changing room, and then back down the hall. "Let's go."

We must have gotten me into my suit in ninety seconds flat. It took him an extra minute because he had to strip and wiggle into the skinsuit first. I kept my eye on the changing room door, but I didn't have any idea what I would say if someone walked in. We're playing doctor?

My faceplate was still spattered with dried blood, which was part of the vague plan: I assumed they would know that the blood meant trouble, and their bug camera, or whatever it was, would be on me as soon as I stepped outside. I had a powerful flashlight, and would turn that on my face, with no other lights. Then wave my arms, jump around, whatever.

We rushed through the safety check and I put two fresh oxygen bottles into the dog I'd bashed up. Disabled the buzzer, and we crowded into the airlock, closed it and cycled it.

We'd agreed not to use the radio. Card signaled for me to touch helmets. "How long?"

"An hour, anyhow." I could walk past Telegraph Hill by then.

"Okay. Watch where you step, clumsy." I hit his arm.

The door opened and I stepped out into the darkness. Card put one foot out on the sand and leaned back against the door. He pantomimed looking at his watch.

I closed my eyes and pointed the light at my face. Bright red through my eyelids; I knew I'd be dazzled blind for a while after I stopped. So after I'd given them a minute of the bloody faceplate I just stood in one place and shined the light out over the plain, waving it around in fast circles, which I hoped would mean "Help!"

I wasn't sure how long it had taken Red to bring me from their habitat level to the cave where he was parked, and then on to here. Maybe two hours? I hadn't been tracking too well. Without a dust storm it might be faster. I pulled on the dog and headed toward the right of Telegraph Hill.

The last thing I expected to happen was this: I hadn't walked twenty yards when Red came zooming up on his weird vehicle and stopped in a great spray of dust.

Card broke radio silence with a justifiable *"Holy shit!"*

Red helped me put the dog on one side and I got into the other and we were off. I looked back and waved at Card, and he waved back. The base shrank really fast and slipped under the horizon.

I looked forward for a moment and then turned away. It was just a little too scary, screaming along a few inches over the ground, missing boulders by a hair. The steering must have been automatic. Or maybe Red had inhuman reflexes. Nothing else about him was all that human.

Except the need to come back and help. He must have been waiting nearby.

It seemed no more than ten or twelve minutes before the thing slowed down and drifted into the slanted cave I remembered. Maybe he had taken a roundabout way before, to hide the fact that they were so close.

We got out the dog and I followed him back down the way we had come a couple of days before. I had to stop twice with coughing fits, and by the time we got to the place where he shed his Mars suit, there was a scary amount of blood.

An odd thing to think, but I wondered whether he would take my body back if I died here. Why should I care?

We went on down, and at the level where the lake was visible, Green was waiting, along with two small ones dressed in white. We went together down to the dark floor and followed blue lines back to what seemed to be the same hospital room where I'd first awakened after the accident.

I slumped down on the pillow, feeling completely drained and about to barf. I unshipped my helmet and took a cautious breath. It smelled like a cold mushroom farm, exactly what I expected.

Red handed me a glass of water and I took it gratefully. Then he picked up my helmet with his two large arms and did a curiously human thing with a small one: he wiped a bit of blood off the inside with one finger, and then lifted it to his mouth to taste it.

"Wait!" I said. "That could be poison to you!"

He set the helmet down. "How nice of you to be concerned," he said, in a voice like a British cube actor.

I just shook my head. After a few seconds I was able to say "What?"

"Many of us can speak English," Green said, "or other of your languages. We've been listening to your radio, television, and cube for two hundred years."

"But…before…you…"

"That was to protect ourselves," Red said. "When we saw you had hurt yourself and I had to bring you here, it was decided that no one would speak a human language in your presence. We are not ready to make contact with humans.

You are a dangerous violent race that tends to destroy what it doesn't understand."

"Not all of us," I said.

"We know that. We were considering various courses of action when we found out you were ill."

"We monitor your colony's communications with Earth," one of the white ones said, "and saw immediately what was happening to you. We all have that breathing fungus soon after we're born. But with us it isn't serious. We have an herb that cures it permanently."

"So…you can fix it?"

Red spread out all four hands. "We are so different from you, in chemistry and biology. The treatment might help you. It might kill you."

"But this crap is sure to kill me if we don't do anything!"

The other white-clad one spoke up. "We don't know. I am called Rezlan, and I am…of a class that studies your people. A scientist, or philosopher.

"The fungus would certainly kill you if it continued to grow. It would fill up your lungs and you couldn't breathe. But we don't know; it never happens to us. Your body may learn to adapt to it, and it would be…illegal? Immoral, improper… for us to experiment on you. If you were to die…I don't know how to say it. Impossible."

"The cure for your ankle was different," Green said. "There was no risk to your life."

I coughed and stared at the spatter of blood on my palm. "But if you don't treat me, and I die? Won't that be the same thing?"

All four of them made a strange buzzing sound. Red patted my shoulder. "Carmen, that's a wonderful joke. 'The same thing.'" He buzzed again, and so did the others.

"Wait," I said, "I'm going to *die* and it's funny?"

"No no no," Green said. "Dying itself isn't funny." Red put his large hands on his potato head and waggled it back and forth, and the others buzzed.

Red tapped his head three times, which set them off again. A natural comedian. "If you have to explain a joke, it isn't funny."

I started to cry, and he took my hand in his small scaly one and patted it. "We are so different. What is funny…is how we here are caught. We don't have a choice. We have to treat you even though we don't know what the outcome will be." He buzzed softly. "But that's not funny to you."

"No!" I tried not to wail. "I can see this part. There's a paradox. You might kill me, trying to help me."

"And that's not funny to you?"

"No, not really. Not at all, really."

"Would it be funny if it was somebody else?"

"Funny? No!"

"What if it was your worst enemy. Would that make you smile?"

"No. I don't have any enemies that bad."

He said something that made the others buzz. I gritted my teeth and tried not to cry. My whole chest hurt, like both lungs held a burning ton of crud, and here I was trying not to barf in front of a bunch of potato-head aliens. "Red. Even if I don't get the joke. Could you do the treatment before I foogly die?"

"Oh, Carmen. It's being prepared. This is…it's a way of dealing with difficult things. We joke. You would say laughing instead of crying." He turned around, evidently looking back the way we had come, though it's hard to tell which way a potato is looking. "It is taking too long, which is part of why we have to laugh. When we have children, it's all at one time, and so they all need the treatment at the same time, a few hundred days later, after they bud. We're trying to grow… it's like trying to find a vegetable out of season? We have to make it grow when it doesn't want to. And make enough for the other younglings in your colony."

"The adults don't get it?"

He did a kind of shrug. "We don't. Or rather, we only get it once, as children. Do you know about whooping cough and measles?"

"What-sels?"

"Measels and whooping cough used to be diseases humans got as children. Before your parents' parents were born. We heard about them on the radio, and they reminded us of this."

A new green-clad small one came through the plastic sheets, holding a stone bowl. She and Red exchanged a few whistles and scrapes. "If you are like us when we are small," he said, "this will make you excrete in every way. So you may want to undress."

How wonderful. Here comes Carmen, the shitting pissing farting burping barfing human sideshow. Don't forget snot and earwax. I got out of the Mars suit and unzipped the skinsuit and stepped out of that. I was cold, and every orifice clenched up tight. "Okay. Let's go."

Red held my right arm with his two large ones, and Green did the same on the left. Not a good sign. The new green one spit into the bowl, and it started to smoke.

She brought the smoking herb under my nose and I tried to get away, but Red and Green held me fast. It was the worst-smelling crap you could ever imagine. I barfed through mouth and nose and then started retching and coughing explosively, horribly, like a cat with a hairball. It did bring up the two fungus things, like furry rotten fruit. I would've barfed again if there had been anything left in my stomach, but I decided to pass out instead.

9. INVASION FROM EARTH

I half woke up, I don't know how much later, with Red tugging gently on my arm. "Carmen," he said, "do you live now? There is a problem."

I grunted something that meant yes, I am alive, but no, I'm not sure I want to be. My throat felt like someone had pulled something scratchy and dead up through it. "Sleep," I said, but he picked me up and started carrying me like a child.

"There are humans from Earth here," he said, speeding up to a run. "They do not understand. They're wrecking everything." He blew through the plastic sheets into the dark hall.

"Red…it's hard to breathe here." He didn't respond, just ran faster, a rippling horse gait. His own breath was coming hard, like sheets of paper being ripped. "Red. I need…suit. Oxygen."

"As we do." We were suddenly in the middle of a crowd—hundreds of them in various sizes and colors—surging up the ramp toward the surface. He said three short words over and over, very loud, and the crowd stopped moving and parted to let us through.

When we went through the next set of doors I could hear air whistling out. On the other side my ears popped with a painful *crack* and I felt cold, colder than I ever had been. "What's happening?"

"Your…humans…have a…thing." He was wheezing before each word. "A tool…that…tears…through."

He set me down gently on the cold rock floor. I shuddered out of control, teeth chattering. No air. Lungs full of nothing but pain. The world was going white. I was starting to die but instead of praying or something I just noticed that the hairs in my nose had frozen and were making a crinkly sound when I tried to breathe.

Red was putting on the plastic layers that made up his Mars suit. He picked me up and I cried out in startled pain— the skin on my right forearm and breast and hip had frozen to the rock— and he held me close with three arms while the fourth did something to seal the plastic. Then he held me with all four arms and crooned something reassuring to weird creatures from another planet. He smelled like a mushroom you wouldn't eat, but I could breathe again.

I was bleeding some from the ripped skin and my lungs and throat still didn't want to work, and I was being hugged to death by a nightmarish singing monster, so rather than put up with it all my body just passed out again.

I woke up to my father fighting with Red, with me in between. Red was trying to hold on to me with his small arms while my father was going after him with some sort of pipe, and he was defending himself with the large arms. "No!" I screamed. "Dad! No!"

Of course he couldn't hear anything in the vacuum, but I guess anyone can lip-read the word "no." He stepped back with an expression on his face that I had never seen. Anguish, I suppose, or rage. Well, here was his daughter, naked and bleeding, in the many arms of a gruesome alien, looking way too much like a movie poster from a century ago.

Taka Wu and Mike Silverman were carrying a spalling laser. "Red," I said, "watch out for the guys with the machine."

"I know," he said, "We've seen you use it underground. That's how they tore up the first set of doors. We can't let them use it again."

It was an interesting standoff. Four big aliens in their plastic-wrap suits. My father and mother and nine other humans in Mars suits, armed with tomato stakes and shovels and one laser, the humans looking kind of pissed off and frightened. The Martians probably were, too. A good thing we hadn't brought any guns to this planet.

Red whispered. "Can you make them leave the machine and follow us?"

"I don't know...they're scared." I mouthed "Mother, Dad," and pointed back the way we had come. "Fol-low us," I said with slow exaggeration. Confined as I was, I couldn't make any sweeping gestures, but I jabbed one forefinger back the way we had come.

Dad stepped forward slowly, his hands palm out. Mother started to follow him. Red shifted me around and held out his hand and my father took it, and held his other one out for mother. She took it and we went crabwise through the dark layers of the second airlock. Then the third and the fourth, and we were on the slope overlooking the lake.

The crowd of aliens we'd left behind was still there, perhaps a daunting sight for mother and Dad. But they held on, and the crowd parted to let us through.

I noticed ice was forming on the edge of the lake. Were we going to kill them all?

"Pardon," Red muttered, and held me so hard I couldn't breathe, while he wiggled out of his suit and left it on the ground, then set me down gently.

It was like walking on ice—on *dry* ice—and my breath came out in plumes. But he and I walked together along the blue line paths, followed by my parents, down to the sanctuary of the white room. Green was waiting there with my skinsuit. I gratefully pulled it on and zipped up. "Boots?"

"Boots," she said, and went back the way we'd come.

"Are you all right?" Red asked.

My father had his helmet off. "These things speak English?"

Red sort of shrugged. "And Chinese, in my case. We've been eavesdropping on you since you discovered radio."

My father fainted dead away.

Green produced this thing that looked like a gray cabbage and held it by Dad's face. I had a vague memory of it being used on me, sort of like an oxygen source. He came around in a minute or so.

"Are you actually Martians?" Mother said. "You can't be."

Red nodded in a jerky way. "We are Martians only the same way you are. We live here. But we came from somewhere else."

"Where?" Dad croaked.

"No time for that. You have to talk to your people. We're losing air and heat, and have to repair the door. Then we have to treat your children. Carmen was near death."

Dad got to his knees and stood up, then stooped to pick up his helmet. "You know how to fix it? The laser damage."

"It knows how to repair itself. But it's like a wound in the body. We have to use stitches or glue to close the hole. Then it grows back."

"So you just need for us to not interfere."

"And help, by showing where the damage is."

He started to put his helmet on. "What about Carmen?"

"Yeah. Where's my suit?"

Red faced me. I realized you could tell that by the little black mouth slit. "You're very weak. You should stay here."

"But—"

"No time to argue. Stay here till we return." All of them but Green went bustling through the airlock.

"So," I said to her. "I guess I'm a hostage."

"My English no good," she said. "Parlez-vous Francais?" I said no. "Nihongo hanasu koto ga dekimasu?"

Probably Japanese, or maybe Martian. "No, sorry." I sat down and waited for the air to run out.

10. ZEN FOR MORONS

Green put a kind of black fibrous poultice on the places where my skin had burned off from the icy ground, and the pain stopped immediately. That raised a big question I couldn't ask, having neglected both French and Japanese in school. But help was on its way.

While I was getting dressed after Green had finished her poulticing, another green one showed up.

"Hello," it said. "I was asked here because I know English. Some English."

"I—I'm glad to meet you. I'm Carmen."

"I know. And you want me to say my name. But you couldn't say it yourself. So give me a name."

"Urn...Robin Hood?"

"I am Robin Hood, then. I am pleased to meet you."

I couldn't think of any pleasantries, so I dove right in: "How come your medicine works for us? My mother says we're unrelated at the most basic level, DNA."

Am I 'DNA' now? I thought I was Robin Hood."

This was not going to be easy. "No. Yes. You're Robin Hood. Why does your medicine work on humans?"

"I don't understand. Why shouldn't it? It's medicine."

So much for the Enigmatic Superior Aliens theory. "Look. You know what a molecule is?"

"I know the word. Very small. Too small to see." He took his big head in two large-arm hands and wiggled it, the way Red did when he was agitated. "Forgive me. Science is not my....there is no word. I can't know science. I don't think any of us can, really. But especially not me."

I gestured at everything. "Then where did *this* all come from? It didn't just *happen.*"

"That's right. It didn't happen. It's always been this way."

I needed a scientist and they sent me a philosopher. Not too bright, either. "Can you ask her?" I pointed to Green. "How can her medicine work, when we're chemically so different?"

"She's not a 'her.' Sometimes she is, and sometimes she's a 'he.' Right now she's a 'what.'"

"Okay. Would you please ask it?"

They exchanged a long series of wheedly-poot-rasp sounds.

"It's something like this," Robin Hood said. "Curing takes intelligence. With Earth humans, the intelligence comes along with the doctor, or scientists. With us, it's in the medicine." He touched the stuff on my breast, which made me jump. "It knows you are different, and works on you differently. It works on the very smallest level."

"Nanotechnology," I said.

"Maybe smaller than that," he said. "As small as chemistry. Intelligent molecules."

"You do know about nanotechnology?"

"Only from TV and the cube." He spidered over to the bed. "Please sit. You make me nervous, balanced there on two legs."

I obliged him. "This is how different we are, Carmen. You know when nanotechnology was discovered."

"End of the twentieth century sometime."

"There's no such knowledge for us. This medicine has always been. Like the living doors that keep the air in. Like the things that make the air, concentrate the oxygen. Somebody made them, but that was so long ago, it was before history. Before we came to Mars."

"Where *did* you come from? When?"

"We would call it Earth, though it's not your Earth, of course. Really far away, really long ago." He paused. "More than ten thousand ares."

A hundred centuries before the Pyramids. "But that's not long enough ago for Mars to be inhabitable. Mars was Mars a million ares ago."

He made an almost human gesture, all four hands palms up. "It could be much longer. At ten thousand ares, history becomes mystery. Our faraway Earth could be a myth. There aren't any space ships lying around.

"What deepens the mystery is that we could never live on Mars, on the surface, but we *could* live on Earth, your Earth. So why were we brought many light years and left on the wrong planet?"

I thought about what Red had said. "Maybe because we're too dangerous."

"That's a theory. Or it might have been dinosaurs. They looked pretty dangerous."

II. SUFFER THE LITTLE CHILDREN

The damage from the laser was repaired in a few hours, and I was bundled back to the colony to be rayed and poked and prodded and interviewed by doctors and scientists. They couldn't find anything wrong with me, human or alien in origin.

"The treatment they gave you sounds like primitive arm-waving," Dr. Jefferson said. "The fact that they don't know why it works is scary."

"They don't know why *anything* works over there. It sounds like it's all hand-me-down science from thousands of years ago."

He nodded and frowned. "You're the only data point we have. If the disease were less serious, I'd introduce it to the kids one at a time, and monitor their progress. But there's no time."

Rather than try to take a bunch of sick children over there, they invited the aliens to come to us. It was Red and Green, logically, with Robin Hood and an amber one following closely behind. I was outside, waiting for them, and escorted Red through the airlock.

Half the adults in the colony seemed crowded into the changing room for a first look at the aliens. There was a lot of whispered conversation while Red worked his way out of his suit.

"It's hot," he said. "The oxygen makes me dizzy. This is less than Earth, though?"

"Slightly less," Dr. Jefferson said. He was in the front of the crowd. "Like living on a mountain."

"It smells strange. But not bad. I can smell your hydroponics."

"Where are children?" Green said as soon as she was out of the suit. "No time talk." She held out her bag of herbs and chemicals and shook it.

The children had been prepared with the idea that these "Martians" were our friends, and had a way to cure them. There were pictures of them and their cave. But a picture of an eight-legged potato-head monstrosity isn't nearly as distressing as the real thing—especially to a room full of children who are terribly ill with something no one can explain (but which they suspect is Martian in origin). So their reaction when Dr. Jefferson walked in with Dargo Solingen and Green was predictable—screaming and crying and, from the ambulatory ones, escape attempts. Of course the doors were locked, with people like me spying in through the windows, looking in on the chaos.

Everybody loves Dr. Jefferson, and almost everybody is afraid of Dargo Solingen, and eventually the combination worked. Green just quietly stood there like Exhibit A, which helped. It takes a while not to think of giant spiders when you see them walk.

They had talked about the possibility of sedating the children, to make the experience less traumatic, but the only data they had about the treatment was my description, and they were afraid that if the children were too relaxed, they wouldn't cough forcefully enough to expel all the crap. Without sedation, the experience might haunt them for the rest of their lives, but at least they would *have* lives.

They wanted to keep the children isolated, and both adults would have to stay in there for a while after the treatment, to make sure they hadn't caught it, unlikely as that seemed.

So the only thing between the child being treated and the ones who were waiting for it was a sheet suspended from the ceiling, and after the first one, they all had heard what they were in for. It was done in age order, youngest to oldest, and at first there was some undignified running around, grabbing the victims and dragging them behind the sheet, where they volubly did the hair-ball performance.

But the children all seemed to sleep peacefully after the thing was over, which calmed most of the others—if they were like me, they hadn't been sleeping much. Card, one of the oldest, who had to wait the longest, pretended to be unconcerned and sleep before the treatment. I know how brave that was of him; he doesn't handle being sick well. As if I did.

The rest of us were mostly crowded into the mess hall, talking with Red and Robin Hood. The other one asked that we call him Fly in Amber, and said that it was his job to remember, so he wouldn't be saying much.

Red said that his job, his function, was hard to describe in human terms. He was sort of like a mayor, a local leader or organizer. He also did things that called for a lot of strength.

Robin Hood said he was being modest; for forty ares he had been a respected leader. When their surveillance device showed that I was in danger of dying, they all looked to Red to make the decision and then act on it.

"It was not a hard decision," he said. "Ever since you landed, we knew that a confrontation was inevitable. I took this opportunity to initiate it, so it would be on our terms. I couldn't know that Carmen would catch this thing, which you call a disease, and bring it back home with her."

"You don't call it a disease?" one of the scientists asked.

"No…I guess in your terms it might be called a 'phase,' a developmental phase. You go from being a young child to being an older child. For us, it's unpleasant but not life-threat-ening."

"It doesn't make sense," the xenologist Howard Jain said. "It's like a human teenager who has acne, transmitting it to a trout. Or even more extreme than that—the trout at least has DNA."

"And you and the trout have a common ancestor," Robin Hood said. "We have no idea what we might have evolved from."

"Did you get the idea of evolution from us?" he asked.

"No, not as a practical matter. We've been cross-breeding plants for a long time. But Darwinism, yes, from you. From your television programs back in the twentieth century."

"Wait," my father said. "How did you build a television receiver in the first place?"

There was a pause, and then Red spoke: "We didn't. It's always been there."

"What?"

"It's a room full of metal spheres, about as tall as I am. They started making noises in the early twentieth century…"

"Those like me remembered them all," Fly in Amber said, "though they were just noises at first."

"…and we knew the signals were from Earth, because we only got them when Earth was in the sky. Then the spheres started showing pictures in mid-century, which gave us vi-sual clues for decoding human language. Then when the cube was developed, they started displaying in three dimensions."

"How long is 'always'?" Howard Jain asked. "How far back does your history go?"

"We don't have history in your sense," Fly in Amber said. "Your history is a record of conflict and change. We have neither, in the normal course of things. A meteorite damaged an outlying area of our home 4,359 ares ago. Otherwise, not much has happened until your radio started talking."

"You have explored Mars more than we have," Robin Hood said, "with your satellites and rovers, and much of what we know about the planet, we got from you. You put your base in this area because of the large frozen lake underground; we assume that's why we were put here, too. But that memory is long gone."

"Some of us have a theory," Red said, "that the memory was somehow suppressed, deliberately erased. What you don't know you can't tell."

"You can't erase a memory," Fly in Amber said.

"*We* can't. The ones who put us here obviously could do many things we can't do."

"You are not a memory expert. I am."

Red's complexion changed slightly, darkening. It probably wasn't the first time they'd had this argument. "One thing I do remember is the 1950s, when television started."

"You're that old!" Jain said.

"Yes, though I was young then. That was during the war between Russia and the United States, the Cold War."

"You have told us this before," Robin Hood said. "Not all of us agree."

Red pushed on. "The United States had an electronic network it called the 'Distant Early Warning System', set up so they would know ahead of time, if Russian bombers were on their way." He paused. "I think that's what we are."

"Warning whom?" Jain said.

"Whoever put us here. We're on Mars instead of Earth because they didn't want you to know about us until you had space flight."

"Until we posed a threat to them," Dad said.

"That's a very human thought." Red paused. "Not to be insulting. But it could also be that they didn't want to influence your development too early. Or it could be that there was no profit in contacting you until you had evolved to this point."

"We wouldn't be any threat to them," Jain said. "If they could come here and set up the underground city we saw, thousands and thousands of years ago, it's hard to imagine what they could do now."

The uncomfortable silence was broken by Maria Rodriguez, who came down from the quarantine area. "They're done now. It looks like all the kids are okay." She looked around at all the serious faces. "I said they're okay. Crisis over."

Actually, it had just begun.

12. THE MARS GIRL

Which is how I became an ambassador to the Martians. Everybody knows they didn't evolve on Mars, but what else are you going to call them?

Red, whose real name is Twenty-one Leader Leader Lifter Leader, suggested that I would be a natural choice as a go-between. I was the first human to meet them, and the fact that they risked exposure by saving my life would help humans accept their good intentions.

On Earth, there was a crash program to orbit a space station, Little Mars, that duplicated the living conditions they were used to. Before my five-year residence on Mars was over, I was taken back there with Red and three other Martians, along with Howard Jain, who would be coordinating research.

Nobody wanted to bring them all the way down to Earth quite yet. A worldwide epidemic of the lung crap wouldn't improve relations, and nobody could say whether they might harbor something even more unpleasant.

So I'm sort of a lab animal, under quarantine and constant medical monitoring, maybe for life. But I'm also an ambassador, the human sidekick for Red and the others. Leaders come up from Earth to make symbolic gestures of friendship, even though it's obviously more about fear than brotherhood. When the Others show up, we want to have a good report card from the Martians.

That will be decades or centuries or even millennia—unless they've figured a way around the speed-of-light speed limit. I'm pretty confident they have. So I might meet them.

A couple of days a week, the Elevator comes up and I meet all kinds of presidents and secretariats and so forth, though there's always a pane of glass between us. More interesting is talking with the scientists and other thinkers who vie for one-week residences here, in the five Spartan rooms the Mars Institute maintains. Sometimes rich people come over from the Hilton to gawk. They pay.

The rest of the time, I spend with Red and the others, trying to learn their language—me, who chickened out of French—and teach them about humans. Meanwhile exercise two hours a day in the thin cold air and Martian gravity, and study for my degrees in xenology. I'll be writing the book some day. Not "a" book. The book.

Every now and then some silly tabloid magazine or show will do the "poor little Mars Girl" routine, about how isolated I am in this goldfish bowl hovering over the Earth, never to have anything like a normal life.

But everybody on Mars is under the same quarantine as I am; everybody who's been exposed to the Martians. I could go back some day and kick Dargo Solingen out of office. Marry some old space pilot.

Who wants a normal life, anyhow?